"I'm not a repressed old maid,"
Stephanie huffed.

Morgan's eyes twinkled with merriment. "I'm glad to hear it. Does that mean you *are* going to have an affair with me?"

"You know perfectly well what I mean," she muttered.

His expression softened. "All your life you've done what was expected of you, what other people wanted. For this one week you're going to do what *you* want."

"Are you sure you're not one of those same people?"

"Only if our desires coincide. Of course I'd like to make love to you—what man wouldn't? You have a siren's body, combined with the face of an angel." His muted voice seemed to vibrate in her midsection. "I'd like to kiss you in every secret place and watch you come alive."

"Morgan, please," she whispered.

"Honesty shouldn't embarrass you."

"That kind does."

"By the end of the week it won't."

Dear Reader:

Stellar is the word that comes to mind for this month's array of writers here at Silhouette **Special Edition**.

Launching a gripping, heart-tugging new "miniseries" is dynamic Lindsay McKenna. *A Question of Honor* (#529) is the premiere novel of *LOVE AND GLORY*, celebrating our men (and women!) in uniform and introducing the Trayherns, a military family as proud and colorful as the American flag. Each *LOVE AND GLORY* novel stands alone, but in the coming months you won't want to miss a one—together they create a family experience as passionate and moving as the American Dream.

Not to be missed, either, are the five other stirring Silhouette **Special Edition** novels on the stands this month, by five more experts on matters of the heart: Barbara Faith, Lynda Trent, Debbie Macomber, Tracy Sinclair and Celeste Hamilton.

Many of you write in asking to see more books about characters you met briefly in a Silhouette **Special Edition,** and many of you request more stories by your favorite Silhouette authors. I hope you'll agree that this month—and every month—Silhouette **Special Edition** offers you the stars!

Best wishes,

Leslie J. Kazanjian,
Senior Editor

TRACY SINCLAIR
King of Hearts

Silhouette Special Edition

Published by Silhouette Books New York

America's Publisher of Contemporary Romance

SILHOUETTE BOOKS
300 East 42nd St., New York, N.Y. 10017

Copyright © 1989 by Tracy Sinclair

ISBN: 0-373-09531-7

First Silhouette Books printing June 1989

Printed in the U.S.A.

Books by Tracy Sinclair

Author of more than twenty-five Silhouette novels, *TRACY SINCLAIR* also contributes to various magazines and newspapers. She says her years as a photojournalist provided the most exciting adventures—and misadventures—of her life. An extensive traveler—from Alaska to South America, and most places in between—and a dedicated volunteer worker—from suicide-prevention programs to English-as-a-second-language lessons—the California resident has accumulated countless fascinating experiences, settings and acquaintances to draw on in plotting her romances.

Chapter One

Why can't we go?" Cindy asked, as she had in an infinite variety of ways for the past hour.

"It isn't fair!" Bambi chimed in.

Although they were both sixteen, their voices had the grating whine of a small child begging to stay up an hour longer. Stephanie Blair suppressed a sigh. How could she last through a whole week of this?

"You know perfectly well your parents wouldn't allow you to go to a disco alone." She tried to keep her voice calmly reasonable.

"What do you think would happen to us?" Cindy asked indignantly. "We aren't babies!"

"I'm sorry, but I'm responsible for seeing that you don't get into any trouble, and I can't allow two young girls to go running around alone at night," Stephanie answered firmly.

"Oh, great! It's bad enough we have to stay in Palm Beach instead of Fort Lauderdale, where the action is. Now you don't want us to have any fun at all!"

"Palm Beach was your parents' choice," Stephanie reminded her.

"Just because Easter week in Fort Lauderdale gets such a bum rap," Cindy grumbled.

Stephanie gazed around the luxurious hotel suite. "Too bad you're so underprivileged," she remarked ironically.

This vacation in Florida had dropped into her lap like a ripe plum. Stephanie enjoyed her job as a language teacher at Miss Waycroft's, an exclusive girls' school, but the Vermont winter had been especially grim. She was delighted when the parents of the two girls had asked her to supervise them on this trip. Cindy and Bambi were two of her favorite students. She hadn't anticipated this kind of trouble.

"If we can't go to discos, what are we supposed to do with ourselves at night?" Bambi demanded.

Stephanie would have been content to have a leisurely dinner in the lovely dining room overlooking the ocean, and then take a walk along the beach. She realized, however, that it was unreasonable to expect that to appeal to a teenager.

"We could go to a movie," she offered tentatively. The sounds of scorn that greeted her suggestion left no doubt about its acceptability.

"I have an idea," Bambi said. "Why don't you come with us to the Pink Panther? Nothing could happen if you're along." Before Stephanie could refuse, she said persuasively, "Besides, you might meet somebody really foxy."

"I know this is hard to believe, but I'm not interested," Stephanie said dryly.

Two pairs of eyes stared at her curiously. Bambi was the one who voiced their thoughts. "Did you have a tragic love affair or something?"

"What on earth gave you that idea?" Stephanie asked in amusement.

"Well, you're a really sexy lady." Bambi assessed her teacher's auburn hair and emerald-green eyes, then dropped to her curved body. "I mean, you still look real young."

Stephanie tried to contain her laughter, realizing that twenty-seven seemed over the hill to these teenagers. "That's very kind of you, Bambi."

"She's right, Miss Blair," Cindy said earnestly. "We all think you're super. None of us can understand why you don't have a steady guy."

Stephanie had wondered about that herself in discouraged moments. She went out on dates, but they weren't soul stirring. Where did you meet the man of your dreams? Or did he exist? Her dates were mostly with professors from the nearby boys' prep school, intelligent young men who were eligible but left a lot to be desired.

"Maybe I'm simply a late bloomer," she said lightly. From the looks on their faces she could tell they thought time was running out.

"Come with us to the disco tonight, anyway," Cindy urged. "If it's a bad scene, we'll leave."

The two young girls looked at her, their smooth faces hopeful. Cindy's blond hair was a mass of ringlets around her face, while Bambi's brown hair spilled down in a long, straight fall. Although they were different in appearance, they shared a heart-tugging innocence. Both were eager to meet life head-on, unaware that they weren't equipped for its pitfalls.

"*Please*, Miss Blair," Bambi urged.

Stephanie's heart melted. "Okay, but we have to come home at a reasonable hour," she warned.

"Anything you say," they agreed hastily.

Stephanie had second thoughts when the cab let them off in front of the Pink Panther a short time later. It wasn't the loud music blaring from the garishly decorated place—she'd expected that—it was the patrons.

The females were dressed in what was almost a uniform, tight miniskirts and blouses that looked like underwear. Although some of them didn't look much older than Cindy and Bambi, they all wore exaggerated makeup and too much jewelry.

The males rivaled them in lack of sartorial splendor. They sported weird hairstyles and body-hugging T-shirts over tight white jeans. Some even wore shorts.

"Girls, I'm not sure," Stephanie began helplessly.

She could have saved her breath. Only physical force would have restrained Cindy and Bambi. Experiencing mild panic, Stephanie watched them merge with the teeming mass on the edge of the dance floor. How had she let herself be talked into this?

"I'll be in the lounge," she called. "Check with me now and then."

She chose one of the stools at the long polished bar, deciding that would give her a better view of the dance floor. Not that she could distinguish much. The large room was in semidarkness, and flashing strobe lights distorted what vision there was.

The cocktail lounge wasn't much brighter. The groups of people sitting in booths and around small tables were indistinct. She could only see the people closest to her clearly. The three men at the far end of the bar were just vaguely discernible. Not that she was interested in them.

When one of the men detached himself from his friends and approached her, Stephanie didn't turn her head.

"May I buy you a drink?" His voice was deep and musical.

"No, thanks," she answered coolly.

"Then would you care to dance?"

"No, thanks," she repeated, searching through the wildly gyrating couples for a glimpse of Bambi and Cindy.

"Don't tell me." Laughter colored his voice. "You're a sociologist studying the ritual behavior of the local natives at play."

"Is that what they're doing? It looks more like a mass exorcism."

"That's possible. Wouldn't you like to join them and cast out a few private devils?"

"I'm used to wrestling with mine in private." She turned to look at him for the first time.

He was older than most of the patrons—perhaps in his middle thirties—but he was dressed in the prevailing casual style. A navy T-shirt spanned his broad chest, and white jeans rode low on his narrow hips. It crossed Stephanie's mind that such a splendid physique wasn't maintained by working in an office. His deep tan was further evidence of an outdoor job, or else he'd been on an extended vacation.

He looked vaguely familiar, but she was sure she would never forget meeting a man like this. Everything about him was impressive—his finely chiseled features, the assurance in his manner, even his regular white teeth. They were almost movie-star quality. The only thing that saved him from being perfect was a tiny, crescent-shaped scar on one high cheekbone.

Amused blue eyes were aware of her scrutiny. He undoubtedly received this reaction a lot, Stephanie thought, annoyed with herself for being struck momentarily speechless.

"Don't let me keep you from dancing," she said hastily.

"I'd rather talk to you, if you don't mind. Won't you let me buy you a drink?" he coaxed.

She didn't see any reason to refuse, since it was better than sitting alone. Besides, the man intrigued her. He certainly didn't have to pick up women in discos. What was he doing there?

"Do you come here often?" she asked, then started to laugh. "I can't believe I just said that."

"Why?"

"It used to be the standard opening gambit at singles' bars—along with what's your sign?"

He looked puzzled. "My sign?"

"Either you're from outer space or you're putting me on."

He hesitated for a moment. "Well, actually I'm not up on all the local jargon."

"That line was used pretty universally until it got laughed out of existence." She looked at him curiously. Although his English was flawless, it was colored by a slight accent she couldn't place. "You're not from around here, are you?"

"No, I'm only visiting."

"Where are you from?"

Instead of answering directly he said, "I should have introduced myself sooner. My name is Morgan Destine."

When he looked at her expectantly, Stephanie had no choice but to give her own name. Before she could question him further, Cindy and Bambi joined them.

The two girls were instantly dazzled. "He looks just like Pierce Brosnan," Cindy said in an aside he overheard.

"Who's Pierce Brosnan?" Morgan asked.

When Cindy flushed with embarrassment, Stephanie explained, "He's a movie and television star." She'd probably noticed the resemblance herself, subconsciously. That must be why he looked familiar.

"Don't you go to the movies?" Bambi asked Morgan in disbelief.

"Mr. Destine has a lot of gaps in his education." Stephanie smiled at him.

His answering smile held intimacy, reinforced by his dark velvet voice. "I'm willing to learn."

The flickering light in his eyes was very masculine. Stephanie felt a warming glow, even though she knew his charm was automatic. It was taken at face value by the girls, however. They were obviously visualizing the start of a romantic affair. It was a notion she had to scotch immediately.

"Are you ready to leave?" she asked briskly.

"We just got here!" They both stared at her incredulously.

"We only came back to check with you, like you said." Having done their duty, they vanished into the crowd.

"Your sisters?" Morgan was looking at her quizzically.

Stephanie shook her head, explaining the situation. "I didn't realize what a responsibility I was taking on. Like tonight. They insisted on coming here, but I have the uncomfortable feeling their parents wouldn't approve."

"Why not? All kids go to discos these days."

"But most of them are more sophisticated. Cindy and Bambi are convinced they're adults, but they've been sheltered all their lives. I went to boarding school myself. Believe me, the real world came as a shock."

"It's a mistake to keep too tight a rein on young people," Morgan remarked. "When they do get their freedom, they tend to abuse it."

"We don't keep them prisoner at Miss Waycroft's," she protested. "They go out on dates."

His eyes twinkled. "With proper young men from a nearby boys' school, I'll wager."

"You must have gone to boarding school, also." She laughed.

He neither confirmed nor denied it. "Let them have fun. They're merely stretching their wings."

"I do want them to have a good time," she said doubtfully.

"Then relax. You're not going to spend your whole vacation worrying about them, are you?"

She sighed. "Probably."

"That would be a terrible waste."

"It isn't the way I imagined it would be," she admitted. "I realize it was naive of me, but I thought we'd go swimming during the day, and maybe take in a movie at night, or stroll around and window-shop. Palm Beach has fabulous boutiques."

He looked at her with a raised eyebrow. "That's your idea of a fun vacation?"

It obviously wasn't his type of thing. "It's been a long, cold winter in Vermont," she said defensively. "I was looking forward to soaking up some sun."

"What about after the sun goes down?"

"Even if I were interested in excitement—which I'm not," she said firmly, "I'm chaperoning two impressionable young girls."

"You think they'd go into shock if you enjoyed yourself?"

"I *am* enjoying myself. Or at least I would be if I could get them out of this place," she muttered.

As though granting her wish, the two girls reappeared. But Stephanie's hopes were dashed with their first words.

"A bunch of kids are going on to another disco," Cindy announced excitedly. "Can we go with them?"

"No, you may not." Stephanie's refusal was more curt than it might have been if she hadn't been smarting under Morgan's veiled derision.

He was convinced that she was a prim little schoolteacher from the sticks. Not that his opinion really mattered. He wasn't the kind of man she'd ever have anything to do with under normal circumstances. He was undeniably attractive, but there was a hint of ruthlessness under his urbane manner that suggested he wouldn't necessarily play by the rules to get what he wanted. She wasn't used to dealing with men like that.

"It isn't any different from this place," Bambi was protesting.

"Then you have no reason to leave."

"You don't want us to have any fun," Cindy said mutinously.

"We didn't have to tell you," Bambi agreed. "We could just have gone."

Stephanie felt assaulted from all sides. She took a deep breath, attempting to regain control. "I can see we need to have a long talk. Perhaps we'd better leave now."

Identical expressions of alarm spread over their faces. "You win," Cindy said hastily. "We'll tell the guys we can't go."

Stephanie watched the girls rejoin two boys who wouldn't have gotten through the front door of Miss Waycroft's school for gentlewomen. The one in shorts had spiked hair that stood up in irregular tufts, and the other wore an earring in one ear. A blond girl standing with them had on a red miniskirt and a white halter that looked like a bra.

"Suddenly, 'a bunch of kids' turned into 'the guys,'" Stephanie said ironically. "Now do you wonder why I feel like I'm on a high wire without a net?"

Morgan laughed. "Your parents were probably just as put off by the things you did and the way you looked when you were a teenager."

"I'll have to admit you're right." She smiled unwillingly. "My sister and I grew up when long, shapeless skirts and no makeup were in style. Our mother was a stunning woman who was sure they must have switched babies on her in the hospital."

"So you see, young people join the mainstream eventually, like their parents before them."

"And learn that their expectations aren't always realized." She sighed unconsciously.

Morgan viewed her mobile face with understanding. "Was it always your ambition to teach?"

"No, I sort of gravitated into it through necessity, but I find it very rewarding."

"I'm sure you do. What did you want to be, though?"

"Something glamorous. When I was very young I dreamed of being an opera singer. The fact that I couldn't carry a tune was a bit of a deterrent." She laughed. "But I thought it was a talent you developed, like good posture."

"We all have our disappointments. I wanted to be a jockey."

Stephanie couldn't help smiling. Since he was over six feet tall, with a powerful though lean frame, his fantasy was as unattainable as hers. "What did you become instead?"

"I went into management."

That meant a desk job, something she would have bet against. "You don't look like a corporate executive," she commented.

"Why not?"

"It's wrong to generalize, but you're so...athletic. I would have guessed a golf or tennis pro. You didn't get that fantastic tan sitting in an office."

"The Florida sun does wonders for office pallor. You'll look like a native, too, after a few days here."

"I can't wait to get out in the sun. The best souvenir of a winter vacation is a golden tan."

"You'd better be careful at first." He gazed appreciatively at her creamy skin.

"I'm not one of those beach potatoes who simply lie there and bake," she assured him. "I intend to go surfing and water skiing."

They discussed the available sports and the best places to pursue them. Stephanie was so interested that she wasn't aware of the passing time. Her original wariness toward Morgan had vanished. His behavior had been scrupulously correct, except for the flicker of admiration in his blue eyes. But as long as he kept it under control, that added a fillip to her enjoyment. Who could object to tribute from a man this blatantly masculine, even if nothing would ever come of it?

"Are you hoping your young ladies will be too tired at night to want to go to discos?" Morgan chuckled. Her plans for the days ahead sounded rather strenuous.

Stephanie was abruptly reminded of her responsibilities. She looked at her watch. "Where are the girls? They haven't checked in for a long time." She swiveled on her stool, searching the frenetic crowd.

"They're out there somewhere, having the time of their lives," he said indulgently.

After staring fruitlessly at the dancers for long moments, Stephanie began to get uneasy. "I can't see them anywhere."

"It's a big room," Morgan soothed.

She spotted the girl in the red miniskirt who had been with the two boys Cindy and Bambi wanted to leave with. "Maybe she knows where they are."

As the girl was about to move onto the dance floor, Stephanie approached her. "Have you seen Cindy and Bambi?"

"Who?"

"The blonde with curly hair and her friend, the small brunette."

"Oh, sure. They split with Deke and Charlie."

Stephanie's palms turned sweaty. "I don't think you know who I mean."

"Sure, I do—the two sorority girls from Hicksville."

"Where did they go?" Stephanie asked in a voice she struggled to keep even.

"The guys said something about going to Whiskey Pete's."

"Where is that?" Stephanie asked tautly.

"I know." Morgan took her arm. "I'll take you there. How long ago did they leave?" he asked the girl.

She shrugged. "Maybe half an hour."

"I can't believe they would do this," Stephanie said numbly as Morgan led her to the door. She was too distracted to see the glance he exchanged with the two men at the end of the bar.

Both men were young, about Morgan's age, with the same splendid physique. One had dark hair and the other blond, but they had the same indefinable quality that set

them apart from the other revelers. It was an air of alert-
ness, as though they were spectators rather than partici-
pants in the merriment. They were completely self-
effacing, however. Even if she hadn't been so distrait,
Stephanie wouldn't have noticed them following her and
Morgan out of the bar.

"I'm going to ground them for the rest of the week,"
she said grimly.

"Aren't you overreacting just a little?" Morgan asked
gently as he helped her into a new but undistinguished sedan.

At the edge of her consciousness was surprise. He
seemed like the sort of man who would drive an expensive
sports car, although nothing about him indicated wealth—
except a subtle aura of assurance that money often con-
veys.

"If they'd disobey a direct order, how do I know what
else they'd do?" she asked.

"Put yourself in their place. How would you have felt
if you were sixteen and a boy asked you to go someplace
that sounded exciting?"

"I wouldn't have gone if I'd expressly been denied permission."

"But suppose you had. What would you have done
when you got there?"

She stared at him uncomprehendingly. "The same thing
I did at the Pink Panther."

"Exactly. They're not kicking over the traces, merely
indulging in a little harmless rebellion against a refusal they
considered unfair."

"You think I was wrong?"

"No, I'm just telling you to go easy on them—and
yourself."

Morgan's reassurance struck a note of sanity. "Maybe you're right. They're really good kids. I'll have to be firm with them, but I'll try to do it calmly."

"That's the spirit." He covered her clenched fingers with his big, warm hand.

The contact was comforting. Morgan was a complete stranger, a man she'd met in a bar only a short time before, yet he inspired confidence. It was gratifying to have an ally when she badly needed one.

"It's awfully good of you to help me find the girls," she said. "I feel guilty about taking you away."

"You needn't. I was about to leave anyway when you showed up." He turned his head and gave her a pulse-raising smile. "You made my whole evening."

"I imagine you could have found something more stimulating than this," she said frankly.

"I can't think of anything."

His deep velvet voice and the gleam in his eyes reminded Stephanie that most things in life came with a price tag. Had it been naive of her to think Morgan was merely being a Good Samaritan?

She glanced out the window at the garish neon signs. The neighborhood they were in was definitely seedy. Video-game arcades and topless nightclubs were sandwiched between bars and cheap hamburger joints.

The sign that read Whiskey Pete's could be seen for blocks, but the place drew attention for other reasons. Two policemen were patting down a man spread-eagled against a wall, and a shore patrol paddy wagon was parked outside.

"Good Lord, what kind of place is this?" Stephanie gasped.

"Not your average Junior League club room," Morgan admitted.

"Forget what I said about being reasonable," she stated tersely. "Those girls are headed for solitary confinement!"

"First we have to find them." As he pulled over to the curb, a taxi stopped and two men got out.

The Pink Panther was a cotillion tea compared to Whiskey Pete's. The large room was crowded with people drinking, dancing and shouting to make themselves heard. Some of the byplay was less than friendly. A few shoving matches were occurring in different parts of the room, but when they involved sailors, men from the shore patrol moved in to break things up before they escalated into a riot.

Stephanie looked around the smoke-filled room, appalled. The carefree, teenage atmosphere of the other disco was missing. Although a lot of very young people were present, most of the patrons were mature, hard-eyed individuals.

"How will we ever find them?" she asked helplessly, peering into the gloom.

"Don't worry," Morgan said soothingly. "If they're here, we'll locate them."

"You think that girl might have been mistaken?" Stephanie was suffering from mixed emotions. This was no place for Bambi and Cindy, but if they weren't here, where were they?

"Let's walk around," he suggested.

As they threaded their way through the tables, a man with a tattoo of a snake on his forearm stood up and blocked their path. "How'd you like to dance, baby?" He looked Stephanie over from head to toe.

"The *lady* is with me." Morgan stressed the term.

The other man seemed inclined to argue until he assessed the glint in Morgan's eyes. He was a large man, not

the kind to back down from a fight, but some implacabil-
ity in Morgan made him pause.

"You're a lucky stiff," he mumbled, sitting down
abruptly.

They had traveled almost the entire room before Stephanie spotted the girls. They were seated at a table with the
two young men from the Pink Panther. One had his hand
clamped around Bambi's wrist, the other had an arm
around Cindy's shoulder. Both girls looked frightened.

"Come on, sugar lips," the boy with the spiked hair was
saying to Cindy. "This will help you loosen up. You're
tense as a virgin." He held a cigarette to her mouth.

"I don't want it," she answered tersely. "Bambi and I
have to get back to the Pink Panther."

"Don't be a nerd. The party's just getting good." He
pulled her close and whispered something in her ear.

As she flinched, Morgan stood over them and said,
"Your watch must be wrong. The party's over." He looked
from Cindy to Bambi. "Are you ready to leave?"

"Oh, yes!" It was a heartfelt chorus from both girls.

"Buzz off, mac. These chicks are with us." The two
boys rose belligerently.

"They just remembered a previous engagement," Morgan answered.

"How'd you like me to clean your clock?" Cindy's date
asked truculently.

Morgan's smile was pleasant. "I suggest you grow up
before you try it."

"Don't mess with me, man!"

As the boy swung at him, Morgan parried the blow and
twisted the boy's arm behind his back, then pushed him
into a chair. When the other boy came to his friend's as-
sistance, Morgan tripped him, sending him sprawling on

the floor. The girls rushed over to Stephanie, wide-eyed with apprehension.

"Take them out to the car," Morgan said quietly as other people converged on the scene, attracted by the conflict.

"Come with us," Stephanie urged. The situation was volatile.

"I'll be along. Do as I say," he ordered.

Stephanie didn't want to leave him, but the fright on the girls' faces was the deciding factor. She hustled them out, feeling badly about deserting Morgan. After all, she'd gotten him into this. He looked well able to take care of himself, but not against overwhelming odds.

As she shepherded the girls out, the two men who had followed them from the Pink Panther moved up to flank Morgan.

"Okay, everybody, settle down," the blond one said. "It was just a friendly dispute, and it's all over."

Anyone who had been spoiling for a fight had second thoughts when they looked at the three men grouped solidly together. They made an intimidating trio.

"I could have handled this," Morgan said with annoyance as the onlookers dispersed.

"I'm sure you could, but this sort of thing is the reason I'm around."

"Ken's right," the dark one agreed. "You can't afford to get mixed up in a barroom brawl."

"Damn," Morgan swore softly. He wheeled sharply and strode out of the sleazy nightclub.

Stephanie was too intent on getting the girls outside to say anything to them. Her restraint vanished once they were safely inside the car.

"How could you deliberately disobey me?" she demanded. "I'm very disappointed in both of you."

"We're sorry, Miss Blair," Cindy said. "We didn't know it would turn out like this."

"Why do you think I said you couldn't go?"

"We'll never do it again," Bambi promised.

"I intend to make sure of that." Stephanie's generous mouth was compressed in a straight line. "At this moment I'm very much inclined to take you home on the earliest plane."

"You wouldn't!" Bambi's face was horrified.

"Even criminals get a second chance," Cindy pleaded.

"I don't care to spend an entire week tracking you down from one tacky bar to another," Stephanie stated. "If it hadn't been for Mr. Destine, I have no idea what I would have done."

"I know what we did was wrong, but if we hadn't gone to the Pink Panther tonight, you wouldn't have met him." Cindy looked at her hopefully. "He's a real hunk."

Stephanie stared at her incredulously. "Am I supposed to consider you did me a favor?"

"Well, he *is* dreamy."

Bambi sighed ecstatically. "I'll bet he can really kiss."

Stephanie recalled having the same thought earlier when Morgan had bent close to her in order to be heard over the din. His mouth was firm, with a sensuous lower lip. She'd wondered fleetingly what it would feel like touching hers. She banished the disturbing thought a second time, drawing a deep breath. The girls mustn't be allowed to distract her. Before she could give them the lecture they deserved, Morgan opened the car door.

"I'm so glad to see you!" She breathed a sigh of relief. "I was worried that a fight would break out when all those people started to crowd around. What happened after we left?"

"They lost interest." He turned to the girls in the back seat. "How does a hot fudge sundae sound?"

"Far out!" they answered in unison.

"You're going to reward them for what they did tonight?" Stephanie asked indignantly.

"I think they've learned their lesson."

"We did," Cindy assured him. "Those guys were yucky."

"From now on you're going to listen to the voice of experience, aren't you?" he asked.

"I guess so," Cindy answered grudgingly.

"A more positive answer would help," Morgan said dryly after a glance at Stephanie's stormy face.

"We've admitted we were wrong, but everybody treats us like children," Cindy burst out mutinously. "Okay, so maybe tonight turned out to be a bummer, but I don't see what's so terrible about trying to get some experience on our own. The only guys we ever meet at school are wimps like Miss Blair goes out with."

"Cindy!" Stephanie exclaimed.

"Well, it's true. All you ever date are those professors from Marshall Prep."

"What's wrong with them?" Stephanie asked.

"They aren't real men like Mr. Destine."

Morgan was struggling to conceal his amusement at the look on Stephanie's face. "Thanks for the compliment, but I'm sure Miss Blair's friends are very, um, virile."

"They couldn't win a pillow fight," Bambi said disdainfully. "Not like you, Mr. Destine. You were super in there tonight."

"Getting into a brawl isn't a mark of manhood," Stephanie remarked tartly.

"You're right. I prefer proving mine in more enjoyable ways," he murmured, too low for the youngsters to overhear.

Her heightened color was the only indication that she'd heard him. "Besides, he didn't go looking for a fight. You two were to blame for what happened tonight."

The girls looked at each other, sorry they'd brought the matter up. Cindy changed the subject hastily. "You must work out a lot to keep that great body, Mr. Destine."

He grinned. "For my age, you mean?"

"You're just the right age," she assured him.

"Don't you think I'm a wee bit old for you?"

"I wasn't talking about myself," she answered demurely.

Fortunately for Stephanie's peace of mind, they arrived at the ice-cream parlor. It was large and brightly lit for a change.

As the girls scampered ahead to get a table she said, "Short of stuffing cotton in their mouths, I don't know what I'm going to do with those two."

"Relax and enjoy them. They're very refreshing."

"You wouldn't think so if *you* were being pushed on someone like a loaf of day-old bread."

"That's something you'll never have to worry about." The glance he gave her held male approval. "They don't approve of your choice in men, that's all."

"Don't be so pleased with yourself. You've seen *their* choices."

He chuckled. "Well, at least I don't have a punk hairdo. Isn't that a point in my favor?"

They joined the girls as Stephanie reflected on how many things she liked about Morgan. Cindy was right. He was very different from the men she dated, or any man she'd ever known, for that matter. Why couldn't they have met someplace where they'd get a chance to know each other, instead of on a brief week's vacation?

The girls were by no means through with their match-making. They were determined to find out everything about Morgan.

"Where are you from, Mr. Destine?" Bambi started the interrogation after they were seated.

"I consider myself a citizen of the world," he answered smoothly.

"Wow, that's deep." After a pause, Cindy asked, "Are you down here alone?"

"More or less."

Stephanie didn't know if he was teasing them or purposely avoiding their questions. She was interested in the answers, but when Bambi stepped over the line she had to stop her.

"I guess you're not married, or you wouldn't have been at the Pink Panther alone tonight. Maybe you have a fiancée at home, though," she commented artlessly.

"That's enough, Bambi," Stephanie ordered. "We do not grill people like cheese sandwiches."

"I'm sorry," Bambi mumbled as Morgan laughed.

"You should be," Stephanie said sternly, although privately she wondered what his answer would have been.

Both girls realized they'd skated as far as possible on thin ice, and the conversation turned to less personal subjects.

It was late when Morgan drove them back to the hotel. The two girls suddenly feigned great fatigue, although it didn't come over them until they reached the lobby. They'd been extremely animated in the car.

"Good night, Mr. Destine." Bambi yawned elaborately. "I'll be asleep before I hit the sack," she predicted.

"Me, too. Thank you," Cindy parroted her friend. "You can stay here and say good-night, Miss Blair. We'll see you in the morning."

Stephanie watched their hasty retreat with a jaundiced eye. "Isn't it amazing how fast the little flowers faded?"

Morgan laughed. "The threat of a lecture has that effect."

"They don't know it, but they've only won a postponement."

"Go easy on them," he advised. "They're just high-spirited kids."

"I can't let them off without a good talking-to," she protested.

"I imagine you'll find them very chastened after their unpleasant experience."

"For about an hour and a half," she observed cynically.

"What you need is some adult companionship. Have dinner with me tomorrow night. We'll drive to a little place I found up the coast, and we won't mention children all evening."

"It sounds heavenly, but I can't." She declined reluctantly.

"You don't know what you're missing. The seafood is fantastic."

A hot dog would have been equally delicious if they could have shared it, but it was impossible under the circumstances. "I can't leave the girls alone."

His gaze went over her classic features, lingering on her softly curved mouth. "I wish you didn't have quite so much integrity, but I have to admire you for it."

"Thanks for everything, Morgan. I'd have been lost without you."

"You would have managed, but I'm glad I was there."
He took her hand and raised it to his lips. "Good night,
Stephanie."

Her hand tingled all the way up in the elevator. The
small gesture might have seemed ridiculous performed by
any other man, but Morgan carried it off with savoir faire.
Maybe it was the custom in his country—wherever that
was. He'd never gotten around to telling her.

Stephanie sighed heavily as she got into bed. She'd never
know now. Morgan hadn't put up much of a struggle when
she turned down his dinner invitation. He wouldn't have
any trouble finding a replacement.

Her eyes were dreamy as she gazed up at the ceiling,
imagining how it could have been. Maybe they would have
gone dancing after dinner. She could picture herself in his
arms, circling the floor slowly, her body responding to the
directions his gave.

As a spreading warmth enveloped her, Stephanie uttered a small sound of exasperation and turned onto her
stomach. Romantic dreams were for teenagers. Morgan
was simply a very pleasant man she'd met in a bar and
would never see again.

Chapter Two

Bambi and Cindy were up and out of the suite before Stephanie was awake the next morning. They could have been eager to get an early start on their vacation, but Stephanie surmised they were avoiding her—in private, anyway. They knew she wouldn't lecture them in public.

The girls were in the pool when Stephanie went downstairs. They were in animated conversation with a boy about their own age. Maybe she should take lessons from them, Stephanie thought in amusement. They certainly had no difficulty finding young men.

After waving a greeting, she selected one of the many empty chaises scattered around. The pool area was relatively deserted at this early hour. Two couples were working on their tans at the shallow end, and an older woman sat at an umbrella table.

As Stephanie was taking a book out of her beach bag, Bambi climbed out of the pool and came over to her.

"You were up early," Stephanie commented. "And so quiet, too. I didn't hear you leave."

"We didn't want to wake you," Bambi answered virtuously.

Stephanie smiled. "That was very thoughtful of you. Have you had breakfast?"

"At the coffee shop." Bambi's face lit up. "We met this neat guy. He's staying here at the hotel."

"That's nice."

"It's great! We're all going water-skiing after lunch." Her voice became diffident. "If that's all right with you."

Stephanie felt a warm rush of affection. "It sounds like a lot of fun."

"You're not coming with us?" Bambi's face reflected her anxiety.

Stephanie laughed. "No, I'll find some other way to amuse myself."

"You're out of sight, Miss Blair." Bambi ran back to the pool and jumped in, sending water splashing over the edge.

A few moments later the older woman walked over and sat on the foot of the chaise next to Stephanie. "Are those two girls with you?"

"Yes. I hope Bambi didn't get you wet."

"No, but I wouldn't have minded if she had."

"You must be very fond of children."

"Not always. I have one I'm ready to put up for adoption at times, but there isn't a large demand for seventeen-year-old boys."

Stephanie glanced toward the pool. "That young man is yours?"

"My one and only. He's usually a joy, but he didn't want to come on this trip with us. Gary was all set to leave for a dude ranch out west when the friend he was going with broke his ankle. Our plans were all made, and we didn't want to leave him home alone.''

"A Florida vacation sounds like a fair exchange.''

The woman sighed. "You'd think so, but Gary's made our lives miserable. I was so delighted when your girls showed up this morning. All of a sudden Palm Beach got better.''

"He made it more attractive for my two, also.''

The woman looked at her curiously. "I don't mean to be inquisitive, but you're too young to be their mother.''

"I'm aging fast.'' Stephanie laughed and explained the situation. "Maybe now we can all start enjoying our vacation.''

The woman introduced herself as Caroline Van Alston. She and her husband were from Pittsburgh, where he practiced law. Stephanie found her good company, and the morning passed enjoyably. Her husband proved to be equally pleasant when he showed up shortly before noon.

They asked Stephanie to join them for lunch, an invitation she accepted. The young people planned to have hamburgers at the snack bar by the pool, and neither needed nor wanted her company.

After lunch the teenagers went water-skiing, and the Van Alstons had a previous engagement. Stephanie was left alone, a prospect she looked forward to at first.

She went for a swim in the ocean and then a long walk along the beach, stopping to pick up interesting shells along the way. The scenery was magnificent, blue sky, aquamarine water and waving green palm trees. Having no one to share it with, however, took a slight edge off the pleasure.

After a while she went back to her chaise by the pool. The wide expanse was crowded now. Groups of people chatted together, but no one paid any attention to Stephanie except the lifeguard. From his perch on a high chair he eyed her slender body with interest. Her pink bikini was relatively modest compared to some, but it displayed her curves admirably.

She glanced around, sizing up the other hotel guests. They were mostly older people. Cindy was right; the younger crowd was in Fort Lauderdale. Stephanie sighed. It might not be a very stimulating week after all, at least for her. She thanked her lucky stars for Gary Van Alston as she opened a book and started to read. The sun and boredom made her drowsy sometime later and she dozed off.

A deep masculine voice woke her. "Don't you know better than to fall asleep in the sun with that magnolia-petal skin of yours?"

She opened her eyes to find a tall, dark man standing over her. "Morgan!" she exclaimed happily. "I didn't expect to see you."

He curved a hand over her shoulder. "It's lucky I got here when I did. You're starting to burn."

Morgan was an awesome sight in brief white shorts that contrasted with his deep tan. His broad chest was lightly covered with black curling hair that formed a V down to his flat stomach. Below the shorts, his legs were long and muscular.

"I don't want to go home lily white," she protested weakly.

"You don't want to spend your whole vacation too burned to enjoy yourself, either." He picked up a gauzy pink beach coat she'd draped over the back of the chaise. "Put this on."

She raised an eyebrow as he guided her arms into the sleeves without waiting for her to do it. "You're very bossy."

He grinned. "I prefer to call myself public-spirited."

Autocratic was closer to the mark, as though Morgan was used to making the decisions. Stephanie regarded him curiously. "Do you have a job with a lot of authority?"

"Let's just say I usually get my own way." He finished buttoning her robe. "Come on, you need to get out of the sun."

He led her to one of the tables on the covered patio that bordered the pool. When they were seated and had given their order for tall drinks, Morgan said, "I was surprised to find you alone. Where are the terrible twins?"

Stephanie told him about their meeting with Gary.

"He must be safe as a bank vault if you let your precious charges go out with him," Morgan teased.

"Actually, he's so completely acceptable that I'm surprised they would consider it."

"Never try to figure out the teenage mind. In any case, now you can have dinner with me tonight."

"I would have expected you to have another date by now."

"I was hoping you'd change your mind."

"Because you always get your own way? If I didn't know better I'd say you planted Gary here," she joked.

"I would have if I'd thought of it." He chuckled. "Is eight o'clock all right?"

"I'd like to say yes, but I'll have to wait and see if the girls have plans."

"I'm sure they do, and their plans don't include you."

"You're probably right." She laughed, recalling the horror on Bambi's face when she thought their day was going to be chaperoned.

"Trust me." Morgan lifted her hand to his lips as he had the previous night.

"That's a charming gesture," she remarked. "I've never had my hand kissed before. You're very good at it."

His white teeth flashed in a grin. "How do you know, if it's a new experience?"

"You do it with such élan. Is it a custom where you come from?"

"It's one of the few ways a man can kiss a beautiful woman he's just met, and not get his face slapped."

"And here I thought it was a mark of respect."

"A man can respect and desire a woman at the same time." Something flickered in his dark blue eyes.

She managed to keep her voice casual in spite of a sudden feeling of breathlessness. "What a civilized way to express desire."

"I can think of more satisfying ones," he murmured.

"I prefer the one you used," she answered primly.

"Whatever you say." His eyes sparkled with wicked amusement at her discomfort. "You got quite a sunburn," he remarked with apparent innocence. "Your cheeks are like wild roses."

"I'll be more careful tomorrow."

"We'll do something that will keep you out of the sun for a day," he promised.

"You'd better not commit yourself," she said carefully. "You might have second thoughts after tonight."

Morgan was a fascinating man, but they clearly had differing relationships in mind. He might as well understand that from the beginning.

"What surprises are you warning me about?" he teased.

"None. That's the whole point. I don't want you to...be disappointed."

He gazed fondly at her pink cheeks. "Cindy was right. You *don't* know anything about men. If I merely wanted a warm body in my bed, one wouldn't be difficult to find."

"I didn't mean..." She stopped, realizing they both knew exactly what she'd meant.

"Those professors you run around with must be a pretty sorry lot to have made you so defensive."

She smiled wryly. "They're rather unimaginative for scholars."

"Too bad. An exquisite woman should be treated with loving care, like the work of art that God made her." His husky voice was sensuous.

Stephanie resisted it with an effort. "Maybe in your circles, but it must be obvious to you that I'm not in your league, Morgan. I'm a small-town schoolteacher."

"A very special one."

She smiled wistfully. "You're almost required to say that."

He shook his head, gazing at her thickly lashed green eyes and the lustrous auburn hair tumbling around her slim shoulders. "I can't believe you have so little ego. Tell me about yourself. Why did you choose to teach in a small town instead of a big city?"

"I didn't have many options after my parents died. I'd gone to Miss Waycroft's myself. We were taught how to write a proper thank-you note, and which side of the plate the fish knife and fork belong on, but not how to scratch and claw in the business world."

"You would have preferred a career in business?"

"I needed a job," she answered tersely.

Morgan looked puzzled. "Miss Waycroft's is a private school, isn't it?"

"And expensive—I know what you're thinking. The explanation is simple. I grew up in the proverbial lap of luxury—a big house, my own convertible, designer clothes. Then my father made a series of bad investments. When he died unexpectedly there was nothing left."

"I'm sorry," Morgan murmured.

"Don't be. He gave me more than most people ever have, including a first-rate education. Unfortunately it was longer on the arts than practicality. I found that out when I had to support myself. The ability to speak several languages fluently doesn't mean much unless you can also type. The job offer from Waycroft was a lifesaver."

"And you've been there ever since." His voice was impassive.

"I like the work. I'm very close to my students." She was angered by the need to defend herself. Her lifestyle might seem tame to a man like Morgan, but it suited her admirably.

Sensing her annoyance, he changed the subject. "Were you an only child?"

"No, I have an older sister, Eloise. She's married and has two adorable little boys." Stephanie laughed a trifle self-consciously. "So now you know all about me."

"Not as much as I'd like to," he answered softly.

"It's your turn," she said quickly. "I've been doing all the talking, probably boring you to tears."

"Not at all. I found it most interesting."

"I'm sure your life story is more so. Where are you from?"

"I was surprised that you knew my background was foreign. Most people never guess. What betrayed me, not knowing my sign?" he joked.

"That was a dead giveaway." She smiled. "But actually it was something about your speech. Not that you have an accent. It's more of a flavor, I guess you could say. As a language teacher my ears are trained to detect nuances."

"What languages do you speak?"

"The popular ones, French, Italian and Spanish."

"Most impressive."

"What's *your* native tongue?"

Before he could tell her, Cindy and Bambi rushed up to their table, bubbling with enthusiasm over their day. Gary trailed a few steps behind, accompanied by another boy about his age.

"We had the most fantastic time," Bambi announced. "You should see Gary water-ski. He's really bad!"

Stephanie gave Morgan an amused look. "That's another colloquialism to add to your list. It means good."

"And we met David down at the dock." Cindy turned to include the unknown young man. "He just got here last night, too, and he's staying next door at the Warwick. Isn't that awesome?"

"To the max," Stephanie agreed.

"We're all going to a barbecue on the beach tonight, and tomorrow we're going to play tennis and take a ride in a glass-bottom boat."

"If we're lucky we might see a shark," Bambi chimed in, and both girls shivered happily.

"Totally gross," Stephanie said indulgently.

Cindy looked sideways at Morgan. "What are you doing tonight, Miss Blair?"

Morgan chuckled, covering Stephanie's hand with his own. "I intend to provide her with excitement."

"All right!" both girls exclaimed in unison. They wheeled around like a couple of skittish ponies and left as abruptly as they'd arrived.

Stephanie withdrew her hand and turned on Morgan indignantly. "Did you have to say that? Now they'll go home and tell the whole school I picked up a man in a bar and had an abandoned affair with him!"

"Anyone can tell your inhibitions wouldn't permit it." He smiled.

She was less than pleased. "In spite of what you think, I don't happen to be a repressed old maid."

His eyes twinkled with merriment. "I'm glad to hear it. Does that mean you *are* going to have an affair with me?"

"You know perfectly well what I mean," she muttered.

His face softened. "You worry too much. In the short time we have together, I hope to make you forget some of that proper etiquette you were brought up on. You need to have some fun."

She looked at him doubtfully. "Do I come across as that much of a prude?"

"Not at all. You're an intelligent, charming woman who's burdened with an overdeveloped sense of duty. All your life you've done what was expected of you, what other people wanted. For this one week you're going to do what *you* want."

She returned his gaze directly. "Are you sure you're not one of those same people?"

"Only if our desires coincide. Of course I'd like to make love to you—what man wouldn't? You have a siren's body, combined with the face of an angel." His muted voice seemed to vibrate inside her midsection. "I'd like to kiss you in every secret place and watch you come alive."

"Morgan, please," she whispered.

"Honesty shouldn't embarrass you," he said gently.

"That kind does."

"It won't by the end of the week," he said confidently.

Stephanie was torn between common sense and the urge to break out of her predictable life. Morgan was right about that. She'd been living too long in a sort of limbo. But a holiday romance wasn't the answer—certainly not with Morgan. He was much too charismatic. She could quite conceivably fall in love with him, and that would be a disaster.

He looked tenderly at her troubled face. "I won't pressure you, honey. This time you're free to make up your own mind."

"You must be pretty sure it will be in your favor or you wouldn't waste a week on me," she commented, still doubtful.

"That's another thing I plan to work on—your ego." He drew her to her feet. "I'll see you at eight. Dress casually."

Stephanie felt a lot more nervous than her teenagers as she got ready for her date that evening. They had dashed out with supreme confidence a short time earlier. But why not? They weren't meeting a man whose potent masculinity and smoky voice could sway any woman's judgment.

Her eyes were wistful as she applied mascara to her long lashes without really paying attention. In her imagination she was seeing a tall, dark man and an auburn-haired woman enjoying the exquisite prelude to love. He was slowly stroking her nude body with his fingertips while his lips trailed a string of kisses from her cheek to her neck and shoulders.

Stephanie caught her breath as her eyes focused on her dreamy face in the mirror. What on earth had gotten into her? She was behaving like the girls at their worst! Morgan would unquestionably be an experienced and satisfactory lover, but she had no intention of validating the fact personally.

When she'd finished dressing in a white linen skirt and a jade-green blouse that matched her eyes, Stephanie went downstairs. A little thrill of anticipation traveled through her veins, in spite of her resolution.

Morgan was waiting for her when she got off the elevator, looking like an elegant stranger. She'd only seen him in jeans and shorts before. Now he wore cream-colored slacks and a matching silk shirt, open at the throat. The lightweight jacket that completed his outfit was expertly tailored to his broad shoulders. With his easy yet regal bearing, he was devastatingly handsome. Several women crossing the lobby turned their heads for a second glance.

"How lovely you look," he said, his eyes lighting with admiration.

"I was thinking the same thing about you," she answered frankly.

He laughed. "That's a nice but unexpected compliment. What happened to the conventional lady who was taught never to make personal remarks?"

"She decided to take your advice and shed a few inhibitions."

"How does it feel?"

"Wonderful!"

"You're an apt pupil," he commented approvingly.

The drive along the coast was very romantic. A full moon made a path of silver across the ocean, illuminating the little wavelets and long breakers that foamed along the sand. Coconut palms were silhouetted against the sky, their fronds waving languidly in the soft breeze.

"I hope you'll like the restaurant we're going to," Morgan remarked. "The food is outstanding, but it isn't the kind of place that attracts tourists."

"I'm sure I'll be pleased. How did you happen to find it?"

"I like to roam around looking for the unusual. I have a whole list of places that are off the beaten track."

"That's rather surprising," she commented.

"Why?"

"You don't seem like the type who enjoys simple pleasures." She studied his faultlessly tailored outfit. "I would think you'd be more at home drinking champagne in some glitzy nightclub."

"That can get tiresome." His voice had a peculiarly flat tone.

"Oh, I don't know. Fancy service isn't all that bad."

"I'm sorry. I should have asked where you wanted to go tonight."

"I was just joking," she said hastily. "Actually I prefer places that aren't pretentious."

They had reached the restaurant, an undistinguished building on a low cliff overlooking the ocean. As Morgan pulled into a parking space in the adjacent lot, a car with two men followed them in and parked some distance away.

The Lobster Trap was a seafood place, as the name implied. It was crowded, but Morgan managed to get a choice table by one of the wide windows that provided a view of the ocean. They postponed looking at the menus while they had a drink and enjoyed the stunning vista outside.

Stephanie gazed at the exotic scene appreciatively. "I can't believe the snow is still knee-deep at home."

"It's hard to imagine when you're in the tropics," he agreed. "Do you ski?"

"Every chance I get. That's one of the few bonuses of winter."

"There's also the scenery. A stark black and white landscape is as beautiful in its way as all this."

"But not after months and months of it."

"I suppose not."

"Does it snow in your country?" she asked.

"Very seldom. Is your drink all right? Would you like a twist of lemon?"

"No, thanks, this is fine."

"I believe I'd like one." He looked around for a waiter. After indicating his request, Morgan touched her face lightly. "Your cheeks are sunburned."

"You should see the rest of me!"

"I'd like to." He smiled.

She ignored that. "When I got out of the shower I was red as a lobster. I only hope it turns to tan instead of peeling. How long did it take you to get yours?" She gazed admiringly at his bronze face and throat. His hands were the same color, with long tapered fingers.

"I have a tan most of the year," he answered.

"So all that poetic appreciation of a snowy winter was just talk," she teased. "You don't have one in your country."

"Not like yours." He reached for the menus the waiter had left. "If you like stone crabs, they're excellent here."

Stephanie knew she wasn't imagining things. Morgan was definitely being evasive. Every time she mentioned anything pertaining to his background, he changed the subject. Why?

"The red snapper is also good," he continued. "All the fish is freshly caught."

"I suppose it would be," she answered absentmindedly.

"If you ever feel like getting up early we can go down and watch the fishing boats come in. Or better yet, we can charter a boat and catch our own. Would you like that?"

"Very much, but chartering a boat sounds expensive. I'd be happy to go on one of those fishing boats that take groups of people."

"Have you ever been on one?"

"No," she admitted.

"You wouldn't like it. They're so crowded you can't tell which line is yours."

"That might be my only way to catch a fish. I'm a novice at the sport."

"Then you need private instruction."

He took it for granted the matter was settled. Stephanie didn't argue any longer, but she was slightly puzzled. Morgan wore elegant clothes and thought nothing of booking an expensive charter, yet he drove a modest car and dined in unassuming restaurants. Not that either of the latter bothered her. It simply didn't add up.

The food was as good as Morgan had promised. They'd both decided on stone crabs, the crustaceans with the large claws that Florida was famous for.

A bowl in the middle of the table was piled high with shells when Stephanie finally sat back with a satisfied sigh. "I can't eat another morsel."

"You must have room for key lime pie," he coaxed. "It's a specialty here. I've made a comprehensive study, and this is the best."

"How can you eat like this and stay so trim?"

"A lot of exercise and good metabolism." His gaze went over her appraisingly. "You don't look as though you have a weight problem, either."

"I will if I keep this up." She laughed. "I'm not one of those dedicated souls who do push-ups and deep-knee bends every morning. Are you?"

"That's boring. I prefer sports."

"What kind?"

"Almost any kind, but especially the ones having to do with water—sailing, surfing, that sort of thing."

"You can't do those all year round, though," she observed. "Unless of course you live somewhere tropical."

"That's true." He signaled to the waiter. "We'd better order our pie before they run out. It's very popular here."

Stephanie waited until the man had cleared the table. When he'd gone she said, "Is there some reason why you change the subject every time you think I'm about to get personal?"

His even teeth showed in a grin. "I'd like nothing better. How personal are you going to get?"

"I'm serious, Morgan," she said crossly.

"My dear Stephanie, what makes you think I'm not? Would you prefer my place or yours?"

Her mouth thinned in annoyance. "Assuming I'd select your place, where would that be? I have no idea where you're staying. I don't know *anything* about you."

"If I'd known that was the only obstacle I'd have been delighted to enlighten you sooner. I'm staying at a rented house on the beach not far from your hotel."

"Are you here for an extended visit?"

"No, I'll be leaving soon."

"To go home?"

He shook his head. "I have to attend a conference in London." His face was filled with amusement. "Would you like to know my itinerary after that?"

Stephanie was suddenly uncomfortably aware that she'd been firing questions at him. "I wasn't trying to pry. It just seemed that you were being evasive."

"I didn't mean to be. What would you like to know?" Before she could ask any questions he continued, "I'm thirty-six, unmarried and in excellent health. I have one brother who's married and has a six-year-old daughter. She is probably the most spoiled child on the face of the earth because her mother doesn't believe in disciplining her."

"How about your brother? Can't he do something?"

Morgan shrugged. "Lydia is a very strong woman. Henri finds it easier to go along with her."

"You two must be very different," Stephanie remarked. She couldn't imagine Morgan allowing his wife to dominate him.

"We are. Henri lacks a goal in life." He frowned briefly. "Sometimes I think it's my fault for not giving him more responsibility, but he hasn't handled it well."

"Are you in business together?"

"Yes, our family business." Morgan's slight pause went unnoticed. Stephanie was too interested in finally hearing some details of his life.

"That can be sticky," she conceded. "Is he older or younger than you?"

"Younger."

"That might be part of it. I remember resenting my sister because she was allowed to do things I wasn't."

"I presume she's older?"

Stephanie nodded. "But only by two years. We're very close now."

"You're fortunate," he remarked neutrally.

Things were evidently different in his case. "You're a very forceful man," she observed a little diffidently. "Perhaps your brother feels he can never be the person you are, so he doesn't try."

"I think that bothers Lydia more than Henri." Morgan's eyes narrowed for a moment, then warmed with a smile. "Do you really find me forceful? I've tried to be on my good behavior."

"I wonder what you're like when you're not," Stephanie mused, almost to herself.

"I'd be happy to show you," he murmured.

"That wasn't the kind of behavior I was referring to," she said reprovingly.

"What then?"

She hesitated an instant. Morgan was a man she wouldn't want to cross. He was charming on the surface, yet she sensed a steely quality underneath. No wonder his brother felt inadequate. Morgan would steamroller any opposition to his will, whether it came from a man or a woman.

He was waiting for an answer, so she finally said, "I wouldn't want to make you angry."

"I don't think you ever could." He took her hand and rubbed his thumb slowly over the soft skin of her wrist. "You're so sweet. I've never met a woman so overwhelmingly lovely, yet so unspoiled."

She laughed to cover the thrill of pleasure his compliment brought. "Cindy and Bambi would dispute that. They think I'm a tyrant."

"I doubt it seriously."

"You should have heard them when I said they had to be in by midnight." She glanced automatically at her watch and was surprised to find it was after eleven. "We'd better go," she said regretfully. "By the time we drive back it will be almost twelve."

"You don't have to tuck them in," he observed mildly.

"No, but I have to be there to see they get back on time. That's the reason their parents are paying for my vacation."

"You're not getting much out of it," he complained.

"That's not true. I've had a wonderful time tonight," she said shyly.

His frown faded as he gazed at her through the flickering candlelight. "This is only the beginning. We have a whole week ahead."

The glow in his eyes lit an answering warmth inside her. If tonight was any indication, an entire week with Morgan should be quite an experience.

The restaurant was almost empty when they left. Only two tables were still occupied. One by a couple who seemed oblivious to anything except each other, the second by two men who were finishing their coffee. In contrast to the loving couple, they looked rather bored.

When she and Morgan arrived back at her hotel, Stephanie was reluctant to see the evening end. "Would you like to come up for a drink?" she asked. "We have one of those little bars in the suite."

"That sounds like an excellent idea."

She hadn't noticed that the girls had left their beach paraphernalia strewn over several chairs. After showing him where the bar was, Stephanie said, "Will you make the drinks while I straighten the living room?"

He watched with a lifted eyebrow as she gathered up straw hats and beach coats. "If you were really a tyrant you'd make them do that themselves."

"I don't mind." She smiled. "They might not be neat, but they're lovable."

He walked over and cradled her chin in his hands. "They must have learned that from you."

Stephanie was suddenly grateful that the girls would be back soon. Morgan was not only powerfully attractive, he was a master at seduction. The desire in his eyes made her quiveringly aware of her own frailty. She wanted to take the small step that would put her in his arms, could imagine the arousing feeling of his mouth moving over hers.

She turned away instead. "You heard their opinion of me," she said brightly. "They don't think I can teach them anything useful."

He let her go. "What you have can't be learned," he said softly.

When she came out of the bedroom, Morgan had selected two miniature bottles of brandy and poured them into snifter glasses. Handing her one, he said, "Shall we take these out on the terrace?"

The lights of the city were a sparkling contrast to the dark ocean murmuring below. Over all, the sky formed a spangled canopy lit by a lemon-yellow moon. It was a scene glamorous enough for an old-time Hollywood movie.

"I don't know which are more beautiful here, the days or the nights," Stephanie commented.

"You don't have to choose." He gently brushed away a long strand of hair that had blown across her face. "You can have it all."

"No one can do that," she said wistfully. "Everything has a price tag."

"Not everything." He drew her into his arms. "The best things in life are the ones you exchange with someone else."

"Morgan, I don't—"

His mouth cut off her words, and after an instinctive protest she relaxed and let her body flow against his. The sensation was everything she'd thought it would be. His lean torso was unyielding. Every hard muscle made her aware of his masculinity. She surrendered to his demands, clinging to him as his kiss became more torrid.

Her lips parted helplessly before the onslaught of his tongue, while his hands caressed her body. She was caught in a whirlpool of desire more powerful than any conscious thought.

"Beautiful Stephanie." His mouth burned a path down her neck. "I knew there was passion under that cool reserve. You're an enchanting combination of fire and ice."

"I've never felt this way before," she whispered faintly.

"My lovely sleeping princess." His fingers stroked her breast sensuously. "You've never had a man worthy of you."

His mouth returned to hers, heightening the pleasure until she existed in a world of pure sensation. Morgan had taken possession of her mind and her body. She was completely under his spell.

When he lifted his head a few moments later, she looked at him uncomprehendingly. He smiled tenderly and combed her ruffled hair with gentle fingers. It was only then that Stephanie heard the high-pitched voices of Bambi and Cindy.

Her whole body flushed with embarrassment as the passion receded. How could she have fallen into Morgan's arms without even a token struggle? He must think she'd invited him up here to make love to her. And if the girls hadn't come home, that's exactly what would have happened! She turned away, trying to compose herself.

Morgan had seen the tortured look on her face. He cupped her cheek in his palm. "It's all right, angel. What happened was perfectly natural."

She pulled away from him. "Not for me, it wasn't."

"Why does it bother you to find out you're a warm, generous woman with normal feelings?"

"I'd rather not talk about it. Would you please leave?"

"Not until you stop feeling guilty over nothing."

"Is that what you call it? You were trying to seduce me!"

"Do you honestly think I would start to make love to you, knowing the girls would return any minute?"

"You weren't exactly making small talk," she muttered.

He smiled. "You're even more innocent than I thought." Framing her face in his palms he said softly,

"When I make love to you it won't be a hurried thing, and there won't be any seduction involved. You'll come to me willingly, and it will be right and beautiful."

"I thought I heard voices." Cindy appeared in the doorway to the terrace. Taking a comprehensive look at them she said, "Oops, I didn't mean to barge in on anything."

"Don't be ridiculous." Stephanie brushed by her into the welcome light of the living room. "Mr. Destine and I were simply having a drink, but he's leaving now."

"He doesn't have to on our account." Cindy gazed at her flushed cheeks with great interest. "We're out of here."

"Sure, stay as long as you like, Mr. Destine." Bambi glanced knowingly over her shoulder as she followed her friend to their bedroom.

"Now see what you've done!" Stephanie exploded after they'd gone. "They're convinced we were making love."

"No, they think we were *about* to," he corrected laughingly.

"That doesn't make it any better. I'm supposed to be setting a good example."

"If they grow up to be like you they'll be very fortunate." He leaned down and kissed her lightly. "Stop worrying about nothing. I'll see you tomorrow around eleven."

She stopped him as he prepared to leave. "I don't think that's a very good idea under the circumstances."

"What circumstances? One kiss?"

Stephanie knew that was an oversimplification. "I'm afraid they're getting the wrong idea," she said miserably.

"If it will ease your mind I'll tell them the truth—that I'd like very much to make love to you, but you turned me down."

"That's all I need," she muttered.

"Are you coming with me tomorrow?"

"Maybe some other time. I really haven't been paying enough attention to the girls." She avoided looking at him.

"Cindy, Bambi, come out here," he ordered.

They popped out so quickly that Stephanie suspected they'd been listening at the door.

"Miss Blair and I are going fishing tomorrow," he said pleasantly. "Will you two be able to entertain yourselves without getting into any trouble?"

"Yes, Mr. Destine," they chorused.

"Then it's all settled." He smiled at Stephanie, leaving her no choice but to tacitly agree.

"He's a real fox," Cindy said admiringly after Morgan had gone. "Were you making out on the balcony?"

"Of course not," Stephanie snapped.

"You passed up a good thing, then," Bambi observed. "I'll bet he can kiss up a storm."

"Oh, go to bed!" Stephanie stalked angrily to her room.

Chapter Three

Stephanie went down to the lobby reluctantly the next morning. A night of thinking about what had happened on the terrace only deepened her feeling of inadequacy when it came to dealing with Morgan.

He could say all that had happened between them was an innocent kiss, but she knew better. It was a shock to discover her own vulnerability. No man had ever evoked the feeling before.

Facing him was awkward, but Morgan made it easy for her. He didn't refer to the night before, through either word or innuendo. By the time they reached the pier and boarded the small boat he'd chartered, Stephanie was a great deal more relaxed. Morgan seemed willing to abide by her terms.

She turned her head to look at him as he squatted on his haunches over the tackle box. Supple muscles rippled along his well-shaped thighs and calves, and the brisk breeze ruffled his thick sable hair. He was a stunning example of a man in his prime. Stephanie sighed unconsciously.

He looked up and smiled. "Are you going to stand there looking gorgeous, or are you going to help me bait the hooks?"

"Only if you're not using anything live."

"Does that mean you're squeamish, or tenderhearted?"

"A little of both," she admitted. "Maybe I'd better just watch."

"Never stand on the sidelines," he chided. "You have to take advantage of everything life has to offer."

Morgan was a living advertisement for his philosophy, she thought. He was so vibrantly alive.

They were well out to sea before two sailors appeared on deck. Stephanie was surprised, not realizing anyone else was aboard. She was even more surprised when she recognized the two men as the ones who had been in the restaurant the night before. Life was certainly full of little coincidences.

She nodded to them pleasantly. "Hello. Lovely day, isn't it?"

Morgan turned around, thinking she was talking to him. A black scowl darkened his face when he saw the two sailors. "I thought I—" He broke off to turn toward the bridge. "Captain Anderson," he called imperiously. "Come down here please."

The captain's face was expressionless when he joined them. "What's the trouble, Mr. Destine?"

"I'd like to know what these men are doing here. I believe we agreed there would be no other passengers."

"Yes, sir, but these men are my, uh, my deckhands."

"We aren't crossing the Atlantic. Why do you need a crew for a few hours of fishing? And why wasn't I informed that you were bringing them aboard?" Morgan's expression was stormy.

"It's a safety regulation," the captain said blandly.

"It's nonsense, that's what it is! What could possibly happen out here in the ocean?"

The two sailors gazed at Morgan impassively, but Stephanie was upset. Although she'd known Morgan only a short time, they'd been together in a number of different situations, and she'd never seen him ruffled. Why was he creating a scene now?

"If it's a rule, you can't expect him to break it," she murmured.

He ground his teeth impotently. "Just *once* I'd like a little privacy."

She stared at him with a puzzled frown. "Don't you think you're making a big deal out of nothing?"

Morgan's rigid features relaxed. "You're right, of course. I apologize. To you, also, gentlemen. Why don't you get us all a beer and then grab a fishing pole?"

Stephanie had to admit that when Morgan made amends he went all out. The sailors seemed to harbor no ill feelings, and the day became a festive one. The men fished alongside them, because the rule about having to carry a crew did seem to be a foolish one. They had nothing else to do.

By the end of the day they'd caught an impressive number of fish. Stephanie was proud that she'd held her own and kept up with the men, in spite of being a novice.

"You fellows might have outnumbered me, but mine's the biggest," she bragged, looking proudly at the large pompano she'd reeled in.

"How would you like to have it for dinner?" Morgan asked.

"Raw?" she asked doubtfully.

"No, stuffed with shrimp and crabmeat."

"Mmm, sounds delicious, but how do you plan to accomplish that?"

He gripped her shoulders, pulling her closer so he could rub noses playfully. "Have I ever disappointed you?"

Her body reacted automatically to his touch, even a chaste one. She moved away, answering lightly, "That's no guarantee for the future."

"Still playing it safe, aren't you? When are you going to start being more adventurous?"

It was late when Morgan dropped Stephanie off at her hotel. They'd made a stop first at a restaurant he'd found that would cook and serve a patron's own catch.

Cindy and Bambi were in the suite watching television, which surprised Stephanie. At this hour they should be rushing around, washing their hair and getting ready for a date with their new boyfriends. They'd been full of plans that morning.

"What time are you going out?" she asked.

"We aren't." Bambi sighed. "Gary's parents are making him go to a dumb wedding with them."

"And David has to pick up his grandmother at the airport and spend the evening with her," Cindy said. "What a bummer."

Stephanie agreed with her. She'd have to break her date with Morgan. "That's too bad," she remarked tepidly.

"Tell me!" Bambi flopped back on the couch. "Where is Mr. Destine taking you tonight?"

"Nowhere. I'll stay here with you."

"That's silly," Cindy protested. "Just because we struck out doesn't mean you have to. One of us might as well get lucky."

"I hope that doesn't mean what it sounds like," Stephanie said ominously. "My relationship with Mr. Destine is one of friendship, nothing more, and I don't appreciate your constant innuendoes."

"I'm sorry, Miss Blair." Cindy instantly regretted her flippant remark.

"We know you wouldn't do anything out of line," Bambi said earnestly.

They were so chastened that Stephanie relented, especially since she didn't share Bambi's confidence. Without the girls to remind her that she had an image to uphold, she might forget that brief encounters were tacky.

Since Stephanie didn't know where to reach him, she couldn't phone Morgan to tell him their date was off. He arrived at the appointed time looking dashingly handsome in white slacks and a navy blazer.

The news of their change in plans didn't bother him. "We'll take the girls with us," he announced casually. "The fish is big enough for everybody. Is that all right with you?" he asked Bambi and Cindy.

"Great!" they agreed.

Stephanie had mixed emotions about his easy acceptance of the situation. It lent weight to her claim that they were merely friends, but she wished—illogically—that he'd shown a little disappointment.

The girls were on their best behavior during dinner. Only once did their frankness make her uncomfortable. It was during a discussion of their future plans, of which they had many.

"I'm going to date a lot of guys, but I'm never going to get married," Bambi announced.

Morgan smiled. "You might change your mind when you meet someone special."

"No, I won't. I intend to have a career."

"You can have both," Stephanie pointed out.

"*You* don't," Bambi answered bluntly.

"Well, I... That's only because I never met anyone I wanted to marry." Stephanie was aware of Morgan's enigmatic eyes watching her.

"Would you leave Miss Waycroft's if you got married?" Cindy asked curiously.

"Not necessarily. I suppose it would depend on the circumstances. If my husband lived in another town, for instance."

"*I* wouldn't change my life for some man," Bambi said scornfully.

Morgan looked at her in amusement. "Not even if it was for the better?"

She considered the matter judiciously. "Well, maybe if he was a millionaire and had a jet plane and bought me lots of clothes and stuff."

"Your values leave a lot to be desired," Stephanie said reprovingly.

"At least she's honest about what she wants," Morgan commented cynically. "Not all women are."

"Forget millionaires," Cindy advised. "They're all old and fat. You're better off staying single like Miss Blair and Mr. Destine. Look at the fun they're having."

"Our condition isn't carved in stone," he remarked dryly. "We could conceivably still hobble down the aisle."

The startled surprise in their eyes amused Stephanie— until they looked from her to Morgan in speculation.

After dinner he suggested they all go swimming, an idea the girls endorsed enthusiastically. The air was balmy, and the night as picturesque as the one before.

"What will you do for bathing trunks?" Bambi asked Morgan as they drove to the hotel. "Are you going skinny-dipping?"

He chuckled at her impudence. "It's an intriguing idea with such a lovely harem, but I always keep a suit in the car."

They had the swimming pool to themselves, which was a good thing because Morgan and the girls alternated between diving off the springboard and racing each other to the shallow end. Stephanie was content to swim languidly, or float on her back and look up at the millions of stars.

She was startled when Morgan surfaced beside her. A moment earlier his glistening body had been arching through the air before slicing the water cleanly.

"You look like a mermaid." His fingers combed through her trailing hair.

"Weren't mermaids blond?"

"I don't believe it was a requirement." He wound a long strand of hair around her throat. "They only had to be sexy, and you certainly fit that description." His eyes traveled over her partially exposed breasts.

She lowered her legs to tread water. "Don't spoil your record now. You've been good all evening."

"I can be even better," he murmured, putting his hands on her waist and drawing her closer.

"Morgan, stop!" She looked nervously over her shoulder.

He laughed. "They won't mind. They approve of me, remember? Besides, you don't have to worry about my trying to make love to you while the youngsters are around." A long forefinger traced the top of her bikini under the water. "The time to worry is when I get you alone."

"You'll have to come to Vermont," she said lightly.

"Is that an invitation?"

"Would you accept?" she countered.

"I'd be crazy not to." His smooth voice was as liquid as the water surrounding them.

Loud cries of joy diverted their attention. Gary had come back from the wedding. After a greeting fit for a returning war hero, the young people settled an important issue. Should Gary put on his swimming trunks, or should they go out somewhere? When the matter was settled both girls swam over to Stephanie.

"We're going to the Trade Winds for hamburgers. Is that okay?" Bambi asked.

"You just had dinner."

"That was hours ago!"

Stephanie looked at the clock on the wall, noting with surprise that it was almost eleven. "All right, but be back by midnight."

"After we get dressed there won't be any time left," they protested indignantly.

"Twelve-thirty, then."

After a little grumbling the girls scrambled out of the pool. Stephanie and Morgan followed their example. The breeze was turning cool.

"You're getting more flexible," he remarked approvingly.

"You're all wearing me down."

"Only the girls. They're evidently more convincing than I am."

"Not necessarily. I'd let you stay up an extra half hour, too, if you asked me," she said demurely.

"What good would it do me? No, don't answer that. I like to live in a dreamworld."

When they reached the suite Stephanie found it difficult to sustain their easy banter. She tried to conceal her tension, however.

"Would you like to shower before you dress?" she asked casually.

"I would, if you don't mind."

"I guess you'd better use my bathroom. I don't like to think what theirs is like."

"I'd suggest we shower together, but I don't suppose it would get me anywhere," he said mischievously.

"You're learning fast," she answered lightly.

When she heard him turn on the shower Stephanie went into her bedroom. Her bathing suit felt clammy, and she wanted to change into a caftan. Secure in the knowledge that she'd have ample notice when the water stopped running, she stripped off her suit and started for the closet.

Without any warning, Morgan came out of the bathroom. Stephanie was caught like a startled doe with nowhere to run. His eyes kindled as he gazed at her slender nude body.

"I thought you were in the shower," she gasped.

"I came out to get my clothes," he answered absently, moving toward her.

She was rooted to the spot, incapable of making a decision. When Morgan was only a few inches away she tried to cover herself. He gently removed her hands, holding them out from her sides.

"Don't be shy, darling. You're as exquisite as I knew you'd be," he said in a voice husky with emotion.

"Let me go, Morgan," she begged. "I didn't mean for this to happen."

"Don't you know it was inevitable?" He released her wrists, but only so he could stroke her breasts.

She drew in her breath sharply at the molten feeling. "Please," she whispered, not sure exactly what she was asking for.

"I've wanted you since the first moment I saw you," he murmured, sliding his hands over the gentle slope of her hips. "Even before I found out how very special you are."

She struggled to resist his powerful attraction, but it was no use. When his warm lips fastened around her nipple she was lost. The thrill that shot through her was like nothing she'd ever experienced. His hands heightened the pleasure as they caressed her slowly, building the excitement.

When he drew her into his arms she quivered at the contact with his lean body. The sensation was electric, scorching her with the heat he was giving forth. She felt herself melting in the crucible of their shared passion.

Morgan lifted her into his arms and carried her to the bed. "My lovely siren, you've cast a spell over me." He knelt over her, staring down with glittering eyes.

When she twisted her legs restlessly and lowered her lashes, he kissed her eyelids tenderly. "Don't be timid with me. I want to look at every enchanting inch of you."

He lowered his head to string a fiery line of kisses down her body while he stroked her thighs with sensual expertise. Her desire mounted at every erotic touch. She reached blindly for him, whispering his name over and over. When his body covered hers, she moved against him in mute entreaty.

"My sweet angel, you want me, don't you?" His lips were a tantalizing fraction from hers.

As she started to tell him how much, a strident sound ripped through the quiet room. It shrilled again, toppling Stephanie from the heights.

"You'd better answer it." Morgan reached for the telephone and handed it to her.

"Hello," she said faintly, when she was able to speak.

"It's me, Cindy. You sound funny. Were you asleep, Miss Blair?"

"No, I... it's all right." Stephanie dragged the spread over her naked body and turned away from Morgan.

"I'm sorry to wake you, but we wanted to know if we can stay an extra half hour. We're really having fun."

"Yes, that will be all right," Stephanie answered tonelessly.

"Gee, thanks! You're the most."

There was silence in the room after she hung up. A long moment passed while she could feel Morgan's eyes on her averted face. Finally he said, "I wish you didn't feel this way."

"Just go," she said in a choked voice.

"Not until we talk about what happened."

"Don't make it worse."

"Why are you so upset? Honest emotion is a lovely, spontaneous thing. It isn't wrong to reach out to another person."

"Men and women regard sex differently," she said stiffly.

"Is that all you think it was?" When she didn't answer, he said regretfully, "I wanted to bring you pleasure, not pain."

He walked into the bathroom and turned off the shower that had been running all that time. A short while later he returned to the bedroom. Stephanie hadn't moved.

He stood over the bed looking down at her. She couldn't see his expression, but his voice was quiet as he said, "I'm sorry, Stephanie."

She got up after she heard the suite door close, feeling battered by the emotions churning inside her. Morgan had taken her to a peak she'd never scaled before. She still ached to feel the full power of his magnificent body, to have him end the torment he'd created with almost casual expertise. That was the thing she had to remember. For him it would have been a night of intimacy like many others, shared with a woman whose name he wouldn't recall after a short time. For her there had to be more.

Stephanie was grateful that the girls had a tennis date at noon the next day. Their enthusiasm for Palm Beach and everything in it was a little hard to take that morning. She breathed a sigh of relief when they eventually made a whirlwind exit.

She wandered over to the window to look glumly out at the scenery that had seemed so beautiful yesterday. It struck her as insipidly boring today. What would she do with herself all day—or for that matter, the rest of the week? They weren't leaving until Sunday, and this was only Tuesday.

When the doorbell rang she sighed. Couldn't the girls ever remember everything the first time, including their key? She went to the door, telling herself not to snap at them. The unexpected sight of Morgan standing in the hall struck her speechless. All she could do was stare at him.

"May I come in?" he asked.

"What are you doing here?" she blurted out finally.

"We have to talk about last night." He came in and closed the door.

She wrapped her arms tightly around her trembling body. "Why did you come? You must know I don't want to see you."

"Because you're blaming yourself needlessly," he said gently.

"I don't want another lecture on the joys of sex!"

He smiled. "That's been well documented. What's at issue is your present reaction."

"I'm sorry I can't match your sophistication," she answered bitterly. "Why don't you look for someone who does? I'm sure you won't have any trouble."

"If that's all I wanted," he agreed.

"You didn't have any doubts last night."

"I've never denied that I want to make love to you. But it hasn't been my primary goal."

"Oh, Morgan, please!"

"You still think that's my one purpose in returning?" He looked at her steadily. "Let's see, not counting Saturday night at the Pink Panther, we've spent two nights and one full day together. That's a lot of hours. If women are that available and I'm as irresistible as you claim, what am I doing here now?"

"Maybe I present a challenge," she answered slowly.

"Or maybe I simply enjoy your company, whether we make love or not." When she ducked her head he said, "I hope you won't let my boorish behavior last night destroy our friendship. I promise not to repeat it."

They both knew he hadn't forced himself on her, but it was considerate of him to pretend he had. "I'd prefer to forget all about it," she murmured.

"That's very generous of you. Now that that's settled, what would you like to do today?"

Stephanie's head shot up. "You're not honestly suggesting we go on seeing each other?"

"Why not?" he asked calmly.

"Because I can't ... I mean, you ..." Her voice trailed off in confusion.

"I'd be very sad to think you don't trust me. I made a promise, and I don't go back on my word."

"It isn't that." She bit her lip nervously. "It's simply out of the question, that's all."

"Give me a reason."

"Well...things wouldn't be the same. Besides, I...I've been neglecting the girls."

It was a patently lame excuse. Morgan looked at her appealingly. "Give me this one afternoon to make amends. We'll take a ride up the coast to a little beach I know. If you're uncomfortable, I'll bring you right back."

He was very persuasive. Without knowing quite how he'd accomplished it, Stephanie found herself in his car. That was the whole trouble, she thought soberly. Morgan could convince her of anything.

The knowledge made her constrained with him, but he acted as though they'd solved all their problems. He kept up a steady flow of disarming conversation as they sped along the highway, ignoring the fact that she said very little.

The traffic thinned after they left the string of beach towns behind. It diminished even more when he turned off onto a two-lane road that wound through stands of palmetto and thickets of sea grapes.

Stephanie was so struck by the quiet and serenity that she made her first spontaneous comment. "You can actually hear the birds sing. This must have been what the whole coast was like before the high-rises sprang up."

"Wait till you see the cove we're headed for. It's completely deserted. You'll feel like Robinson Crusoe."

She turned her head to look at him curiously. "You're a real loner, aren't you?"

"Why do you say that?"

"You prefer out-of-the-way places, and you like privacy." She was thinking of the fuss he'd made about the two sailors on their fishing trip.

"Everyone's entitled to a little privacy," he answered evenly. "Would you like to be surrounded by people every minute?"

"No," she admitted. "I need to be alone sometimes."

"Exactly," he said a trifle grimly as he pulled off the road and parked on the shoulder.

A crescent-shaped beach was directly below the overhang, invisible from the highway. It was sheltered by jutting spits of land that broke the even flow of beach at that point.

"It does look deserted," Stephanie exclaimed. "Do you think pirates put in here in the old days?"

He smiled. "What better place to count their pieces of eight in seclusion?"

"Let's go down and see if they dropped any."

The ocean was like a blue coverlet with an ermine border. It formed a colorful contrast to the smooth white sand marked only by the tracks of birds. They spread out a blanket and stripped off their outer clothes. Morgan had told Stephanie to wear a bathing suit underneath.

The water was a perfect temperature, just cool enough to be invigorating. They swam and dived for shells, gliding among tiny, brightly colored fish, alone in a tropical paradise. The only sign of civilization was another car parked behind Morgan's. But fortunately, whoever owned it had business elsewhere.

Morgan had brought suntan lotion for Stephanie. After they'd dried off he handed her the bottle. "Better put some of this on. You're getting a nice tan, but you can still burn."

"Okay, I'll do your back, and you can do mine."

He smiled. "That's the best offer I've had all week, but I don't need any. I'm already as tan as I can get."

"It keeps your skin from drying out. Turn around."

She squirted the scented liquid into her palm, then smoothed it over the broad expanse of his shoulders and back. Her offer had been entirely innocent, but as she traced the impressive muscles under his smooth skin, her energetic movements slowed unconsciously. The firm texture of his supple body gave her tactile pleasure. It was like fondling a magnificent sculpture that had magically come to life.

Morgan arched away from her with an indrawn breath. "All right, it's your turn now."

She reluctantly handed over the bottle and stretched out on her stomach. Instead of using her gentle touch, he rubbed her back briskly.

"Mmm, that feels good. You'd make a great masseur. Do my legs, too," she instructed.

His firm strokes on her calves were satisfying, but when he separated her legs slightly and moved up to her thighs, Stephanie had second thoughts. His rhythm had slowed to a tempo more suitable for a caress, and her body was reacting in an all too familiar way.

Before she could accuse him of breaking his promise he said, "All done. Your back is oiled like a sardine. You can do your own front."

Stephanie was grateful that she hadn't made a fool of herself. Morgan didn't have any designs on her anymore. He really did have only friendship in mind. The insight should have been more reassuring than it was.

Outside of that one incident—which Morgan wasn't even aware of—the day was a pure delight. They were back on their old footing of easy companionship. Underneath was a current of sexual awareness, but that was no different, either. A frank attraction had always existed between them.

It could have created awkwardness after what had happened the night before, but Morgan handled the situation with his usual grace. He didn't avoid touching her; that would have been pointed. He took her hand while they romped in the surf, and he brushed sand off her stomach. Every contact was casual, though, with no sensual overtones.

When they were lying on the blanket after a refreshing swim Stephanie remarked, "You have a superb stroke. Have you ever taken part in competitions?"

"Only with my brother, which wasn't fair since he was younger and smaller." He gazed pensively out at the horizon. "If I'd been more mature at the time I'd have let him win once in a while."

"He'd have known you were throwing the race."

"Maybe not. I've often wondered if always being second is the reason for his lack of interest in assuming responsibility."

"He's married and has a family," she pointed out.

Morgan smiled derisively. "That's true. And Lydia has enough ambition for both of them."

Stephanie gathered that he didn't care a great deal for his sister-in-law. "Do you see much of them?" she asked delicately.

"More than I could wish at times. They live at the—they live near me."

She was about to ask where that was when a big raindrop splattered on her shoulder. A sudden tropical squall had blown up. The rain would stop as speedily as it had started, but since it was late afternoon by then, they tumbled everything into the blanket and made a dash for the car.

During the drive back to the hotel, Morgan said, "What would you like to do tonight? I've been making all the decisions. It's your turn to choose."

"Have you exhausted your supply of little out-of-the way places?" she teased.

His face was expressionless as he turned his head to look at her. "I suppose they have been a little tame. Perhaps it's time we sought out the bright lights."

"I was only joking." She was sorry he'd taken it as a criticism. "I've enjoyed every minute."

"I hope so, but it was selfish of me. Tonight we'll go to a nightclub."

"You said I got my choice," she reminded him. "Do you know what I'd really prefer? There's an old Hitchcock movie on television." She knew because she'd expected to spend the evening alone watching it. "I'm tired of big dinners. I'd like to order something light from room service and see the movie again."

"You'd rather do that than go out on the town?"

"It was only a thought," she said quickly. "I guess it sounds boring to you. Any place you pick will be fine."

He covered her hand tightly with his. "Have I ever told you that you're an enchanting lady? I can't think of anything I'd rather do tonight."

Stephanie had been making up her mind about something on the drive back. When they reached the hotel she said, "You don't have to go home unless you want to. You can use my shower." It was her way of putting the past behind them.

He understood her motive. "That's a good idea, as long as I already have my clothes with me," he answered casually.

The suite was a beehive of activity for a time as Morgan, Bambi and Cindy each showered. Stephanie took hers

ast. When she emerged from the bedroom with clean hair
and glowing skin, Morgan was mixing drinks. The girls
were clustered around him, seeking his masculine advice.
They'd bestowed their unqualified stamp of approval.

"Mr. Destine says kissing is all right if you really like a
guy," Bambi announced as Stephanie joined them.

"I only said kissing," he warned.

"I got the message, nothing heavy. How do you feel
about French kissing?"

"Personally, you mean?" He grinned.

"No, I know *you* do it."

"Bambi!" Stephanie gasped.

"I don't know why you get so bent out of shape when
we talk about sex," Bambi complained.

"It's a very important part of the relationship between
men and women," Cindy declared, coming to her friend's
defense. "We want to get the male viewpoint. You know,
like what turns guys on."

"Right. What attracted you to Miss Blair?" Bambi
asked Morgan.

"A number of things." His eyes softened as he gazed at
the nimbus of bright hair surrounding Stephanie's flower-
like face. "Her beauty, of course, but it was more than
that. She had a sweet air of vulnerability that's very rare
these days. I thought she deserved someone who would be
gentle with her, and I wanted to be that man." His voice
flowed like a deep current, drawing her to him.

"Far out!" Both girls were staring at him with dazzled
eyes.

"So don't be too quick about bestowing your favors."
His tone was normal when he turned back to the girls.
"You might be giving them to a man who is only inter-
ested in using you."

"Thank you," Stephanie said after the girls had left the room. "You probably did more to set them straight than a dozen lectures I could have given them."

"That's because they think I have more experience than you," he teased.

They'd be so right, she thought silently. Morgan must have brought untold pleasure to many women who hadn't followed the advice he gave the girls. Yet today had changed her mind about his interest in women being merely sexual. He was a finer person than that. Was she being foolish?

Even as she asked herself the question, Stephanie knew the answer. Morgan was beginning to mean more to her every day. If she allowed him to come any closer, she might not be able to walk away at the end of the week with a fond farewell. It would be difficult enough as it was. And he hadn't indicated they had any future together.

Stephanie refused to let discouragement take hold. She was determined to live for the moment, which was special as always. They sat on the couch together and watched television in the softly darkened room. Morgan put his arm around her, and Stephanie rested her head on his solid shoulder. A glow of happiness filled her, even though contentment could have escalated into ecstasy.

Morgan left after the movie was over. As she walked him to the door Stephanie asked, "What are we doing tomorrow?"

"I'm afraid I can't see you. I'll be tied up both day and night."

Under her disappointment was embarrassment that she'd simply taken it for granted they had a date. Morgan had no obligation to spend all his time with her. "Well, have a good time," she said brightly.

"I don't expect to, but it's something that can't be avoided. How about Thursday? Perhaps we can find another secluded cove."

"I hope so." Her heart bounded back to its rightful place. Maybe she should have played harder to get, but Stephanie had no intention of doing so. Half the week was gone already.

She managed to amuse herself all day, but the evening was dull. Cindy and Bambi were off on their tireless pursuits, and Stephanie was left to a solitary dinner and a long, boring night. She considered going to a movie, then rejected the idea in favor of television. It wouldn't be as much fun as watching with Morgan, but then, nothing was.

Before turning to a dramatic show, she decided to watch the news. It was shameful that she hadn't even read a newspaper since she got there.

The world news was somber, but the local news lightened things up. A team of reporters was describing a charity event.

"We're coming to you live from the Palm Room of the Sea Drift Hotel, where the annual Founders' Day Ball is being held," the male member of the duo announced. "All of Palm Beach society is here tonight. Isn't that right, Cathy?"

"That's correct, Bruce. It's a glittering spectacle. The jewels on the ladies are worth a king's ransom."

"A nice turn of phrase, considering the guest of honor. Would you say most of the women are hoping to dance with King Morgantrelle? If that's what you call him."

"His complete title is His Royal Highness, King Phillipe de Morgantrelle, House of Destine."

"That's quite a mouthful."

"He's quite a man," she gushed. "The biggest catch—wait a minute. Isn't that the king entering the ballroom now?"

Stephanie had been about to change the channel when she was caught by the familiarity of the names Morgantrelle and Destine. She stared at the screen in disbelief as the camera panned to Morgan. On his arm was a stunning woman with a smug expression on her face.

He looked different in a white dinner jacket and black trousers, remote somehow, with a regal, slightly bored expression on his handsome face. But she couldn't mistake those chiseled features or that long, lean body.

"That's the Countess Blenville-Saxe-Martin with him," the female newscaster was saying. "She's the chairwoman of this event."

"I'm glad we got a glimpse of the king, because we have to switch back to the newsroom now," Bruce announced. "Stay tuned for more coverage at eleven."

Stephanie turned off the set and stared numbly at the blank screen. Why hadn't Morgan told her who he was? And what was he doing with her in the first place, when he should have been spending his time with his society friends?

Gradually her bewilderment turned to anger. Morgan was acting out his own version of the prince and the pauper. It amused him to pick up a commoner in a bar and give her a big whirl. That was the reason he always took her to little-known places where he wouldn't be recognized. Who would expect to find a king at the Pink Panther or the Lobster Trap? He was ashamed of being seen with her!

All the pieces of the puzzle started falling in place—the nondescript car, his evasiveness about where he was from, the two men who turned up everywhere. They must be his bodyguards. That was probably their car on the bluff yesterday.

Stephanie's cheeks flamed as she imagined what they must have thought. They'd undoubtedly been witness to countless of Morgan's little dalliances. It didn't matter that they were wrong in her case. She'd never forgive Morgan for his deception, never!

Stephanie continued to fuel her anger, because underneath was a feeling of desolation.

Chapter Four

A sleepless night did nothing to improve Stephanie's frame of mind. She was moody and restless the next morning.

Morgan had never given her his telephone number, and now she knew why. It meant she would have to see him again, though, much as she loathed the idea. Her only hope was that he wouldn't keep their date that day. He'd returned to his normal environment last night, so maybe that meant he'd had his little laugh.

She was convinced of the fact when he didn't show up at the time they'd agreed on. Morgan was usually very punctual. His appearance a half hour later was an unwelcome surprise—at least that's what she told herself, attributing the quickened beat of her heart to annoyance.

"Sorry I'm late, angel." His easy manner was the same as always.

Her eyes glittered with suppressed anger. "Did you oversleep after your big night out?"

He looked at her warily. "No, I had some business to attend to this morning. I would have called, but I kept hoping to get away."

"You don't have to explain to me, Your Highness."

Morgan's face held a mixture of emotions. "How did you find out?"

"You were prominently featured on the nightly news. We colonials get quite excited over royalty."

He sighed. "I suppose I should have told you."

"That would have spoiled all the fun, wouldn't it?" she asked tautly. "It was much more amusing to find out how the peasants live."

"Don't talk that way," he said sharply. "I never patronized you."

"No, you were quite charming. You pretended to enjoy the simple pleasures."

"I *did* enjoy them, but mostly because I was with you."

"Yet you made sure nobody knew about it. That was the reason you took me to obscure little places where you wouldn't be recognized. It wouldn't do to be seen with someone who works for a living," she said bitterly.

"Is that what you think of me?" His face set in autocratic lines.

"Don't try to deny it! What other explanation is there?"

"I'll try to excuse you, because you have no idea what my life is like."

"I *saw* what it's like. Those people did everything but blow trumpets when you walked in. Did you oblige all the ladies who wanted to dance with you? Or did you select them by rank?"

"I don't deserve this from you." A white line around Morgan's mouth showed how furious he was. "What have I ever done to give you the impression that I'm a snob?"

"How about being ashamed to be seen with me?"

"You can't possibly believe such an idiotic thing." As she stiffened indignantly he said, "The very opposite is true. I wanted to keep you all to myself."

"How gullible do you think I am?" she demanded.

Morgan sighed, his anger dissipating. "Let me try to explain. I was very attracted to you that first night. If I'd told you who I was we'd never have gotten to know each other. Everyone treats me like some sort of freak when they find out."

"Scarcely. They trip over each other to get near you. I saw it last night."

"Exactly. A bunch of strangers. Nobody cares about *me*. They just want to tell their friends they had dinner with the King of Verlaine. *That's* why I seek out unpretentious places where people accept me for myself. Some like me and some don't, but at least it's because of how I act, not who I am."

Stephanie wanted to believe him, but she didn't trust her reasons. "If that were true you could have told me after we'd gotten to know each other."

"I was tempted, but I was afraid it would change our relationship."

Her eyes slid away from his. "We don't have one."

"Our friendship, then. I've seen too many people become uncomfortable around me when they found out my identity."

"You've had these little adventures before?" she asked bleakly.

Morgan's smile relieved the strain on his face. "Only with drinking buddies and fishermen, people like that.

Never with a beautiful woman whose good opinion I value very much.''

She didn't believe him for a moment. "Well, it was nice while it lasted. If it's any consolation to you, I don't plan to tell anyone I had dinner with the King of Verlaine. They wouldn't believe me, anyway."

"Can't you forgive me?" he pleaded.

"Sure." She looked searchingly at his handsome face as though to memorize it, although there was no need. "I'll never forget you, Morgan."

"That sounds so final."

"It is," she answered simply.

"You don't believe a word I've said, do you?"

She didn't, but further argument would only be painful. "Yes, I do, but you're right about the truth changing things."

He smiled wryly. "You're a bit of a snob, yourself."

"Don't try to turn the tables," she said indignantly, forgetting her good resolutions. "I'm sorry if you're not through playing out your fantasy, but you'll have to find another Cinderella."

He gazed at her with an impassive expression. "I'm invited to a very social party tonight. I had no intention of going, but I've changed my mind. Will you do me the honor of attending it with me?"

"Certainly not! Do you think I'm a child to be placated by a party?"

"Are you afraid you won't fit in?" he taunted.

"My manners are at least as good as that bleached blonde you made an entrance with last night—and maybe better," she stormed.

"We'll see," he answered maddeningly.

"You mean you doubt it?" she asked in outrage.

"You're the one who seems to be insecure."

Stephanie abruptly realized that she was being manipulated. "Forget it! You're not using me to salve your conscience."

"It isn't hurting. You're the one who made accusations. You say I'm ashamed of you. I'm going to prove you're wrong."

"That isn't necessary," she said stiffly. "It no longer matters."

"It does to me. You've impugned my character. The least you can do is give me a chance to absolve myself."

"Why won't you just forget the whole thing?" she asked wretchedly.

His eyes were soft as he gazed at her downcast lashes. The tenderness vanished when she raised her eyes. "My honor is important to me. After you attend the party with me tonight and resolve your doubts, I'll leave you alone—if that's what you want."

Morgan was suddenly a stranger. The warm, teasing man she'd known had disappeared. In his place was an imperious autocrat who was vaguely intimidating.

"Morgan, this is . . ." She stopped to compose herself. "Even if I agreed to go with you, I don't have anything to wear."

It was such an unexpectedly female excuse that he smothered a smile. His face was once more austere as he said, "I'll buy you a gown."

"I'm not a charity case," she flared.

"As you like," he answered indifferently. "It doesn't matter to me what you wear. Just be ready at eight o'clock." He stalked out the door before she could argue the matter further.

Stephanie spent a long time trying to think of ways to get out of the date, but it was hopeless. She could simply be out when he came to call for her, yet that was only a temporary solution. Morgan would track her down sooner or later, and Stephanie didn't like to think about the way he'd voice his displeasure over being stood up.

Since there was no way out, she concentrated on the immediate problem of what to wear that evening. It was an obvious impossibility to match the clothes and jewels the other women would appear in, but she wasn't about to look like some little waif Morgan had befriended, either.

What she'd told him was true, however. She really hadn't brought a suitable gown. Who would have thought she'd need one? The only solution was to go shopping. Stephanie's jaw set grimly. She would buy something utterly smashing, no matter how much it cost.

Red would have suited her defiant mood, but it wasn't a good color with her auburn hair. She settled on white, which created an equally dramatic effect. The little slip of a dress was slinky, sexy and expensive. She gulped at the price, then resolutely ignored it. Her pride was at stake, and that couldn't be measured in money.

When she returned from her shopping trip, a note from the girls informed her that Bambi and Cindy, along with their dates, had gone to a twilight pop concert in Miami with Gary's parents. That made things easier. If they'd seen the new gown they'd have asked endless questions, and Stephanie wasn't up to explanations. With any luck, the girls would never find out Morgan's true identity.

She spent a great deal of time over her appearance, applying a luminous foundation, mascara, eye shadow and blusher to highlight her cheekbones. To go with her glamorous makeup she created an intricate hairdo, fastening the sides of her long hair at the crown with a rhinestone clip. It might not have been diamonds, but it was quite effective nonetheless.

Getting ready had taken all her concentration, but when eight o'clock neared, Stephanie started to tense up. The evening was going to be stressful, but Morgan mustn't notice any chinks in her armor. When the bell rang she took several deep breaths before answering the door with cool composure.

The dazzled look in Morgan's eyes was reward for all her labor, although he masked it immediately. His gaze traveled over her almost clinically. "I see you found something to wear."

She repressed her own annoyance under a like indifference. "A little thing that was on sale. I didn't want to disgrace you completely."

His teeth clamped together. "Shall we go?"

"If you insist."

They made the drive in silence except for one short exchange. When Stephanie noticed the car following them she said, "You might as well have had your bodyguards ride with us."

"They aren't bodyguards," he answered curtly. "Jacques is my aide, and Ken Coulter is with your State Department."

"Whatever," she answered dismissively. "Their function is to keep you out of trouble."

A flash of Morgan's old humor surfaced as he remarked, "You've made their job easy this week."

She turned her head to stare out the window so he wouldn't see her heightened color.

Their destination was a sprawling mansion facing the ocean. It was lit up like a birthday cake, and a loud babel of voices floated out through the open windows. Parking attendants were waiting to take the guests' expensive cars after obsequiously helping the occupants out. They were almost openly disdainful of Morgan's modest sedan, which seemed to amuse him.

The greeting he got inside was quite different. People converged from every direction, all with avid gleams in their eyes. Stephanie watched in amazement as these obviously privileged people fawned like teenage fans over a rock star.

The hostess was an impressive silver-haired matron. "I can't tell you how thrilled I am that you changed your mind about attending our little soirée," she gushed.

"It's indeed an honor," an older man, presumably her husband, agreed.

"Good evening, Your Highness." A woman in a dazzling diamond necklace pushed forward. "We met at the charity ball last night. I do hope you'll reconsider about having lunch on our yacht. Any time that's convenient for you."

"Unfortunately my time is completely scheduled," Morgan answered smoothly. He looked around for Stephanie, who had been backing away unobtrusively. Stretching out a long arm, he pulled her to his side. "I'd like you all to meet my very dear friend, Stephanie Blair."

The focus of attention changed suddenly as everyone looked at her speculatively. She felt like a frog being prepared for dissection. The penetrating glances assessed her gown, her hairdo, everything about her.

"So nice to meet you," their hostess said, a trifle absentmindedly.

Stephanie hadn't spent years at Miss Waycroft's for nothing. Her carefully modulated voice gave no hint of her true feelings when she responded, "I'm delighted to be here."

"If you'll excuse us, I'll get Miss Blair a drink." Morgan's hand on her elbow propelled her through the crowd.

They didn't get far. More people waylaid Morgan with reminders that they'd met, or introduced themselves if they hadn't. He was pressed to accept invitations, to lend his name to good causes. Everyone wanted something.

Morgan was unfailingly charming, but Stephanie sensed his rebellion—and began to understand it. If these people wanted to bask in his reflected glory, why didn't they talk about the stock market, or deep-sea fishing, or the merits of football over soccer? Even the weather would be preferable to this mindless adulation.

He took advantage of a brief respite while they walked to the buffet table to ask her sardonically, "Are you enjoying yourself?"

She wasn't quite ready to forgive him yet for his deception. "I will be after I've had something to eat."

The table was unbelievably lavish, covered with every kind of delicacy surrounding an impressive centerpiece of orchids. Stephanie had just taken a bite of a large prawn when their hostess joined them.

"I've been neglecting you shamefully," she said to Morgan. "Especially since your companion doesn't seem to know anyone here." What she meant was, no one knew *Stephanie*.

"That's quite understandable," Morgan answered blandly. "Miss Blair is from Vermont."

"How interesting. I don't believe I know anyone from there."

He smiled. "You do now."

"Oh…yes, of course." She turned to Stephanie with an innocent air. "What does one do with oneself in Vermont? Culturally, I mean."

Stephanie's mouth was full, so Morgan answered for her. "Miss Blair teaches languages at Miss Waycroft's school for girls."

"Really?" Her gaze swept over Stephanie, evaluating the expensive gown, registering her lack of jewelry, puzzling over the conflicting signals. "I do admire young people who devote their time to others instead of frittering away their days in frivolous pursuits," she finally said tentatively.

As Stephanie's eyes started to glitter Morgan replied, "Miss Blair isn't a dilettante. She has to work for a living. That's why we have so much in common." He gave Stephanie a melting smile. "So few people understand what it's like to have obligations."

The core of resentment inside Stephanie melted as she gained insight into Morgan's life. Who wouldn't want to escape from these superficial people? She felt deeply ashamed of her suspicions, and at the same time proud that he had chosen her as an alternative. Had she ruined everything with her accusations?

"I'm sorry," she murmured.

"How sorry?" His eyes lit with a teasing light.

The older woman realized she'd made a tactical error when she witnessed the undercurrent between them. "Do let me introduce Miss Blair around. Everyone is so anxious to meet her."

That was the last thing Stephanie wanted. "Do you mind if I wash my hands first? I seem to have cocktail sauce all over them."

"You're good at this," Morgan murmured in her ear.

"I paid attention at Miss Waycroft's," she murmured back.

The powder room was crowded. Elegantly gowned women were gossiping while they repaired their makeup. Stephanie's entrance went unnoticed.

"She isn't one of us," a stunning brunette remarked as she combed her already smooth hair. "Where do you suppose he found her?"

"Who knows? I guess even kings aren't particular when they get the urge," her friend remarked.

"That's not very kind, Daphne," a woman with a sweet face protested. "She's beautiful enough to attract any man."

"Phillipe isn't any man. He wouldn't bother with a little nobody unless she was sensational in bed."

Stephanie paused in the doorway, appalled at the crudeness and cruelty of these pillars of society. The inadvertent sound she made gave her away. Before she could back out quietly, they noticed her presence.

She drew herself up to her full height and lifted her chin. "Don't let me interrupt. I thought I was in the *ladies* room, but evidently I made a mistake."

She walked back to Morgan with a stiff back and a grim expression. He was surrounded by the inevitable group of sycophants. When she joined him he put his arm around her waist. Her rigid body communicated the tension she felt, and he looked at her questioningly.

"Is anything wrong?"

"My tolerance isn't as high as yours," she answered caustically. "Would you please take me home?"

"I thought you'd never ask." His teeth showed in a white grin.

"I'm sorry you didn't have a good time," he remarked when they were in the car.

"The Marquis de Sade wouldn't have had a good time at that party," she stormed. "Although they were his kind of people."

"You wouldn't care to be around them every day?"

"Open-heart surgery would be preferable."

"Interesting," Morgan mused. "You had enough after a couple of hours, yet you can't understand how I could feel the same way."

"You might have told me," she said slowly.

"Would you have believed me if you hadn't experienced it for yourself?"

"I suppose not," she confessed. "How do you stand it?"

"It isn't always this bad. Usually my contacts are quite stimulating, although the ideal situation is to meet people without any preconceptions on their part."

"That's deceptive, though," she said uncertainly.

"Could we have had as much fun together?" He turned his head to look at her. "We did have fun, didn't we, Stephanie?"

"Yes," she answered softly. "I'm almost sorry I found out."

"I'm sorry it happened the way it did, but I'm glad in another way. I've been wanting to tell you about my country. I think you'd like it."

"I've read a little bit about Verlaine, but not very much."

"It's a small principality, but our roots go back hundreds of years. And unlike many of the other European countries that still have royal families, ours actually governs. The House of Destine has ruled for centuries. I'm not a playboy monarch."

"You haven't exactly been tending to business this week."

"Even a king gets time off for good behavior." He smiled. "Although this has been a working vacation. I signed papers and sent off dispatches in the morning while you were still snuggled in bed, and after I came back a night I dealt with the day's accumulation of work."

That meant he'd had to make time to be with her. The knowledge was immensely gratifying. "Can't you delegate some responsibility?" she asked.

"I've tried to urge my brother to become more involved. After all, he's second in line until I marry and have children. He should be prepared to take over if anything should happen to me."

Morgan drove onto a turnoff overlooking the beach and cut the motor. His profile, gilded by the moonlight, was like the head of some perfectly sculpted Greek god.

"Don't you have an obligation to marry and produce an heir to the throne?" Stephanie asked.

"I'm very dedicated to my country, but not to the extent of marrying someone I don't love."

"You must be awfully hard to please," she commented lightly.

His expression was unreadable in the darkness. "I could say the same about you. What are you looking for in a man?"

"My case is different," she evaded. "It doesn't matter if I ever marry."

"That doesn't answer my question."

"I'm not sure I can." She glanced out over the moonlit water. "People don't consciously search for a mate. If you're lucky enough to find the right one, it just happens."

"Exactly," he said with satisfaction. "One day when you least expect it, someone absolutely perfect enters your life. You just need to have faith and be patient."

"At least you won't have any trouble persuading her to marry you," she said wistfully.

"I'm not so sure. My wife will have responsibilities. Not every woman would be willing to accept them."

"Name one who wouldn't," Stephanie scoffed.

"How about you?" he asked casually. "Would you like to be a queen? Remember, it has its pluses and minuses."

Morgan would be the plus; she couldn't think of any minuses. "The average woman couldn't even conceive of what it would be like," she answered dismissively. "But you wouldn't marry an average woman, so the question is academic. Any suitable candidates will be well trained for the job."

"You make it sound so romantic," he mocked.

"Well, you have to admit you're not free to choose just anyone."

"That's not strictly true, but I wouldn't want just anyone. I've dreamed of a woman so exquisite she makes my breath stop, and so much in love with me that she doesn't care who I am."

His husky voice evoked a picture Stephanie didn't want to contemplate. Morgan would find his dream girl, but it was painful to hear him describe her.

"You were going to tell me about Verlaine," she said abruptly.

After a short pause he said, "It's a small country, quite beautiful, with forests and streams. One of the rivers runs through the heart of the city where I live."

"Like Amsterdam?"

"Nothing quite that grand. More like the little village of Bruges in Belgium. We also have a number of castles, some in ruins and most reputed to be haunted."

"Have you ever seen a ghost?"

He chuckled. "Not personally, but they're quite a tourist attraction." His face sobered. "We need all the tourists we can get, unfortunately."

"Don't you want people to visit Verlaine?"

"Very much, but I don't want tourism to be our principal attraction. That makes for an unstable economy. I've been traveling widely to promote our other industries."

"What are they?"

"We're an agricultural land, for one thing. The mild weather lends itself to year-round farming. We also have small but valuable mineral deposits. That's the word I want to get out."

Stephanie listened, enthralled as Morgan described a little jewel of a place, rich in cultural heritage and natural beauty.

"It sounds almost too perfect to be true," she commented with an unconscious sigh. "Like a modern Shangri-La."

"I can't guarantee that you'll never get older, but we have other attractions. Why don't you come for a visit?"

"Maybe I will some day," she answered vaguely.

"When?"

"I don't know, when I save up enough money." She laughed lightly. "By that time you won't even remember my name."

"I could never forget you, Stephanie," he answered quietly.

She was filled with a pervading sadness. Morgan would forget all too quickly, but she wouldn't. This week was going to color all her subsequent relationships. Would she ever find anyone to equal him? If only Morgan was an ordinary man. But he wasn't.

"I guess you'd better take me home now," she said tonelessly.

The dashboard clock read only ten-thirty, but there was no sense in prolonging their parting. It wouldn't get any easier.

Stephanie was surprised to find the girls there when she and Morgan returned to the suite. Her surprise was echoed by theirs when they saw how she was dressed.

"You look fabulous!" Bambi gasped. "Where did you get that foxy outfit?"

"I bought it. How was your pop concert?" Stephanie tried to change the subject without much hope of success—and she was right.

"It was okay." Bambi dismissed the evening indifferently. "Where have you been all dressed up like that?"

"We went to a party. Aren't you two home rather early?"

"The concert was over at ten, and the Van Alstons brought us right home. A real bummer," Cindy complained. "What are you doing home at this hour?"

"It isn't that early," Stephanie said.

"Sure it is. Things are just starting to jump." Bambi looked hopefully at her. "Since you're all dressed up, why don't we go to a disco? How about it, Mr. Destine? You don't go to bed this early."

"Not usually," he admitted.

"Well, then?"

"You've had a full enough evening," Stephanie said hastily. She couldn't bear another round of the girls' efforts at matchmaking, not tonight of all nights.

Morgan noted the signs of strain on her face. As the girls started to protest he said, "Perhaps tomorrow night if Miss Blair doesn't have something she'd rather do."

Stephanie turned a startled face to him. "You expect us to go on seeing each other as though nothing had happened?"

The eyes of both girls opened wide. "What happened?" they chorused.

"Nothing." Stephanie instantly regretted her incautious words.

"Come on! You can't leave us dangling."

Stephanie realized she was trapped. "I simply found out...I mean, Mr. Destine isn't what he..." Her voice trailed off.

The girls looked at each other knowingly. "I told you so," Bambi said. "He's married."

Cindy sighed. "I guess he was too good to be true."

Morgan laughed. "I hope you guess better in class."

"You *aren't* married?" Cindy asked hopefully.

"Not even engaged."

"Then what did Miss Blair find out about you that's so terrible?"

"Don't you think you ought to tell them?" he asked Stephanie.

"No!" They really would tell this story to the whole school!

"That's not fair," Cindy protested.

"It wouldn't matter to us," Bambi said earnestly. "We know you're one of the good guys. I'm sure whatever you did wasn't your fault."

"That's very sweet of you," he said gently. "I wish everyone could be as forgiving."

"Mr. Destine didn't *do* anything," Stephanie said tersely, knowing his remark was aimed at her. "He simply neglected to give us his real name."

The girls looked puzzled. "What is it?"

"He's usually addressed as His Royal Highness, King Phillipe de Morgantrelle. Mr. Destine is the King of Verlaine."

Cindy's mouth dropped open as she stared at Morgan. "You're a real, honest-to-goodness king?"

"With a crown and everything?" Bambi looked equally dazzled.

"I haven't worn it in a long time, but it's around the place somewhere." He smiled.

"I can't believe it!" Cindy exclaimed. "Why didn't you tell us?"

"That's a rather sore subject," he answered, slanting a glance at Stephanie.

"Can we come to visit you?"

"Where is Verlaine?"

"Will you send us a picture wearing your crown?"

Their questions tumbled over each other as Stephanie knew they would. Morgan fielded them good-naturedly, but finally he called a halt.

"How would you two like to go to bed so I can have a word with Miss Blair before I leave?"

"Are you going to ask her to visit you in Verlaine?" Bambi asked.

"I'm going to insist on it."

"Wow, that's heavy!"

"Good night," he said firmly.

"Good night, Your Highness."

Cindy unexpectedly dropped an awkward little curtsy. Bambi followed her example after a moment, then they both ran off giggling.

"That wasn't so bad, was it?" he asked Stephanie.

"Not for you, but Miss Waycroft's will never be the same. Especially if you send them an autographed picture."

"I intend to—in my crown." He grinned. "I think I have an old sword around someplace, too. Would they like that?"

"Does a seal eat fish? They'll be insufferable."

"They're nice kids," he said fondly. "I'm going to miss them."

That reminded Stephanie of what brief time remained. "I can't believe the week is almost over."

"We have three days left."

"Only two," she corrected. "The girls and I have a noon flight on Sunday."

He groaned. "That only leaves us one full day to ourselves. I'm committed to a reception at my home on Saturday night."

Stephanie was disappointed, but that was still one more day than she'd anticipated. "We'll just say our goodbyes on Friday night instead of Saturday," she answered, attempting to keep her tone light.

He looked at her consideringly. "Could I persuade you to act as my hostess Saturday night?"

"Oh, no, Morgan, I don't think so."

"It won't be the same people. I'm having some government representatives and quite a few leaders of industry. This reception isn't strictly social, it's important to my country. That's the reason I can't postpone it."

"I wouldn't expect you to."

"We could still be together, though. It will only last for a few hours, and then we can go out to dinner."

"We can do that anyway. I'll wait for you." In spite of her former objections, she couldn't turn down these last precious few hours.

"I'd really like you to be there," he coaxed. "If only to see that my official life isn't always grim."

"I'm sure it isn't, or you couldn't be so well adjusted."

"Come and see anyway," he urged.

She shook her head. "You must know that anyone you pay the slightest attention to is put under a microscope. If

I acted as your hostess, those important people might get the wrong impression.''

"Those people have more on their minds than that. They'd only wonder about you if you couldn't put two words together to form a sentence."

"That might very well be the case. I don't know much about world trade and international agreements.''

"You'll ask intelligent questions,'' he said confidently.

"I wish I believed in myself as much as you do.''

"Perhaps that's part of your charm.'' He took her hands and gazed deeply into her eyes. "You're a unique person, and you don't even know it.''

Stephanie wished with all her heart that she was everything he wanted in a woman, because she'd fallen in love with Morgan. It was useless to call it mere sexual attraction. This was the man she wanted to spend the rest of her life with. Wasn't that ironic? She couldn't have picked anyone farther out of reach.

He looked tenderly at her, misunderstanding the reason for her troubled expression. "You don't have to make up your mind now. Let's decide what we'll do tomorrow. Would you like to have a picnic on our private beach? In the evening we'll take in a floor show at a nightclub.''

That meant people recognizing Morgan and coming over to their table. She didn't want to share the brief time they had left together. "Why don't we go to the movies instead?''

He looked at her searchingly. "You can't still think I'm ashamed to be seen with you.''

"No, I just want one last day to pretend things are the way they were,'' she answered wistfully.

"Can't you accept me for what I am?''

"It's a little difficult,'' she admitted.

"I'm the same person I was." He cupped her chin in his palm and lifted her face to his. "A man who's powerfully attracted to you. You feel something for me, too, don't you, Stephanie?"

Without waiting for an answer he took her in his arms. Although she knew it was folly, her body flowed against his without protest. How could she resist when this was what she wanted so desperately?

Morgan's mouth was urgent, parting her lips for a deep exploration that left her clinging to him as the one fixed object in a spinning world. His hands heightened the heady pleasure, caressing, tantalizing, feeding her desire until she trembled in his arms.

"How can I let you go?" he muttered after dragging his mouth away and burying his face in her hair.

The words brought reality. He would leave her because they belonged in different worlds. She summoned the strength to draw away. "You'd better go," she murmured.

His muted laugh had a shaky sound. "You're right. My self-control isn't limitless." He put his hands on her shoulders to hold her a safe distance away while he kissed her cheek. "Sweet dreams, little Stephanie."

She remained in a kind of trance after he left. Until the girls came rushing out of their room.

"We heard him leave."

"Did he ask you to stay here with him?"

"Wait till the kids at school hear about this!"

"Did he tell you he loved you?"

Their excited questions and comments finally penetrated Stephanie's self-absorption. She struggled for her normal composure. "You're both being utterly ridiculous. I've told you Mr. Destine and I are merely friends—

actually only acquaintances. I don't expect to see or hear from him again after we leave here."

"I'll bet you will," Bambi declared. "He's crazy about you, anyone can see that."

"Just think, if you married him you'd be a queen." Cindy sighed ecstatically.

"Kings don't marry commoners," Stephanie answered somberly.

"How about that English king who gave up his throne for the woman he loved? And what about Prince Ranier? He married a movie star."

"I'm not a movie star. I'm a schoolteacher from a small town," Stephanie said evenly. "On Monday morning I'll be back in the classroom, and Mr. Destine will be spending his time with someone else."

"Didn't he say anything about wanting to see you again after this week?" Cindy asked wistfully.

"No, he didn't." Stephanie's eyes were bleak. "I'm going to bed now. I suggest you two do the same."

Chapter Five

Friday was a bittersweet kind of day. Stephanie and Morgan picnicked on their private beach and swam in the crystal-clear water. They talked easily and fell into companionable silences. On the surface it was a day like the others they'd spent together that week, but for Stephanie there was an undercurrent of sadness.

They went to the movies that evening and ate popcorn like all the other couples around them. Not once did either of them refer to Morgan's status. It wasn't until he brought her home that he mentioned the following night's reception.

"I hope you've changed your mind about tomorrow night," he said at her door.

"I'd really rather not, Morgan."

"Won't you come as a favor to me? I've never asked you for anything before."

"I'm only thinking of what's best for you," she said hesitantly.

"*You're* the best thing that's ever happened to me." He clasped both her hands.

She was powerless to refuse him anything when he touched her, however chastely. Against her better judgment she gave in.

Stephanie took a taxi to the reception the next night after assuring Morgan it made better sense than having him call for her. He couldn't risk being late for his own party.

The rented house he'd referred to so casually was actually an extensive estate overlooking the ocean. It was surrounded by a high wall with an electric gate that stood open now. Guards were stopping each luxury car to check the invitations of the occupants before allowing them entry. The tight security was another sobering reminder that Morgan wasn't an ordinary man.

As Stephanie paused at the entrance to the crowded living room, Morgan left the group he was with and came toward her.

"I was afraid you weren't coming," he said.

"I'm sorry to be late. The traffic was horrendous."

"It doesn't matter as long as you're here." His eyes glowed as he gazed at her. "You look lovely."

She was wearing the dress she'd bought for the other party. "In this old thing?" She smiled impishly.

"In anything—or nothing," he teased.

As her color rose he took her hand and led her around the room, introducing her to the other guests. They were an impressive collection of men and women who held high positions in their respective fields. Stephanie found the conversation intriguing to listen to, but she didn't venture any opinions. When Morgan left her side she felt abandoned in a rarefied environment. Especially when the people she was with politely included her.

"I understand you're a teacher, Miss Blair," an older man remarked. "What is your special field?"

"I teach languages."

He nodded approvingly. "I've always felt we don't put enough emphasis on that segment of education. It's shameful that children in other countries are fluent in many languages while most of us speak only our own tongue."

"That's scarcely fair, Charles," a stunning woman protested. "The people in Europe, for instance, have a geographical advantage. In the space of a relatively few miles they're in another country where they can practice their conversational skills. It's the only way to become fluent, but we don't have that opportunity. Don't you agree, Miss Blair?"

"To a certain extent," Stephanie answered hesitantly. "I think that could be remedied if we really had the desire."

"In what way?" the man asked with interest.

"Our country is filled with people of foreign descent who speak their own language as well as ours, yet we automatically speak to them in English. We pass up opportunities that are often right next door."

"Wouldn't it be considered patronizing, since they're fellow Americans?" the woman asked doubtfully.

"Not at all, she's absolutely right," the man answered for her.

Stephanie's face was animated as they discussed the pros and cons of her idea. She was so engrossed that she failed to miss Morgan, or notice him watching her from a distance with a look of satisfaction on his handsome face.

He returned to steer her unobtrusively from one group to another, then quietly leave her. She soon gained confidence and discovered that she was enjoying herself immensely.

The time sped by. When a few guests started to leave, Stephanie could hardly believe it was almost nine o'clock. The party broke up soon after.

"What marvelously stimulating people," she exclaimed to Morgan when they were alone.

"I thought you might enjoy them."

"I did. It was a wonderful evening! I don't feel sorry for you anymore."

He raised one dark eyebrow. "I didn't know you did."

"You played on my sympathies," she accused. "Pretending all your nights were as dreary as that other one."

"I merely said those were an occasional, necessary evil," he corrected. "I seem to remember telling you it wasn't always that bad."

"Well, what else was I to think when you spent all your time this week with me and the girls?"

"Stephanie, we have to—" He broke off as a servant entered the room.

"Will you require anything further this evening, Your Highness?" the man asked.

"No thank you, Hoskins. That will be all."

After the butler left, Stephanie remarked, "They're certainly efficient. You'd never know there'd been a party in here." The room had been unobtrusively cleared of glasses and cocktail napkins.

"Yes, they've been very satisfactory." Morgan looked at his watch. "Are you getting hungry?"

"Not really. I ate a lot of those delicious hors d'oeuvres. But I'm ready whenever you are."

"Let's have a drink first." He poured two glasses from a bottle of champagne that was sitting in a silver wine cooler.

She accepted the crystal flute he handed her and sank contentedly onto one of the satin striped couches. "This is the part of a party I like best—talking about it afterward. That Mrs. Creighton is charming, isn't she? And so intelligent. Tell me about her."

"You're right, she's brilliant. Besides being active politically, she's an eminent criminal attorney."

"That must be a fascinating field. Everybody here tonight does something important."

"Including you."

She smiled. "You're awfully good for my ego."

"I told you I'd bolster it by the end of the week."

Stephanie stared down at her glass, watching the bubbles rise like tiny comets traveling through sunlight. "Will you be staying here much longer after we leave?"

"Only a few days. Then I go to London, as I told you."

"Better pack your woollies," she remarked brightly. "It will be quite a change from Palm Beach."

"I don't expect to be there very long. I'm due back in Verlaine for the flower festival."

"That sounds nice. What is it?"

"Every year we have a festival to mark the beginning of spring. The houses and storefronts are decorated with garlands of daffodils and tulips, and our main park is turned into a fairground. It's a three-day affair culminating in a parade, with fireworks in the evening."

"It must be very colorful, almost like an operetta."

"The camera shops do a big business. Tourists snap everything, including local dogs and lampposts."

"Not doing what comes naturally, I hope."

"We don't practice censorship." He chuckled.

"Do you have any pictures of the festival?"

"There might be some in our publicity brochures."

"Could you show me one? I'd like to see what Verlaine looks like."

"Jacques might have some, but he isn't here right now."

Stephanie realized this was the first time Morgan's aide hadn't been a shadowy presence in the background. "Where is he? I would have thought he'd be here tonight."

"I insisted that he take a few hours off. He'll be back on the job when we go to dinner." Morgan sighed.

"It must be...inconvenient...to have someone watching every move you make," she observed.

He viewed her prim face with amusement. "Only my public movements. I manage to have some degree of privacy...when the occasion demands it."

She was sorry she'd brought the matter up. "Can't you find the brochures without him?" she asked hurriedly.

"I suppose I could try, but you don't know what my desk looks like," he warned.

"I'll help you," she coaxed.

Morgan had improvised an office in a corner of his bedroom. The room was so massive that the clutter was only a small, jarring note in the pearly perfection of the master suite. Everything was done in white.

One end of the room was furnished as a luxurious sitting area with a down sofa and deep chairs. A canopied bed dominated the other end of the room, trailing gauzy draperies. The stark whiteness of the furnishings was relieved by huge bowls of irises and peonies that provided vivid splashes of color.

Stephanie gazed around appraisingly. "This is a decorator's dream, but it doesn't really look like you."

He made a face. "You're so right, but I didn't have a choice. Fortunately it's only temporary. I'll be home soon."

"What is your palace like?"

"I'll try to find some pictures to show you."

He finally unearthed a brochure sandwiched in among untidy piles of papers. They sat on the couch together while Morgan proudly displayed the attractions of his country.

One photo was of a flower-filled meadow with sheep and a picturesquely dressed shepherd. Another showed people water-skiing on a beautiful blue lake. Finally he pointed to a sprawling stone castle surrounded by acres of lawn. Flags flew from the battlements, and sentries stood guard on either side of a massive portal.

"This is Ravenna Castle," he said with pardonable pride. "It's been continuously occupied by members of the House of Destine for many centuries."

"That's where you live? It looks intimidating."

"It isn't really. It's a lot more comfortable than this place."

"I thought castles were supposed to be drafty places where the wind moans down the chimney, and things go bump in the night."

"You've been watching too many horror movies. Ravenna is a home, not a museum. My quarters have furniture you can be comfortable on, and there are usually a couple of dogs lying in the middle of the floor. You learn to be careful not to trip over them."

"I love dogs. What kind do you have?"

He smiled reminiscently. "One of every breed. People send me the pick of their litters, and I can't very well turn them down. I think at last count we had something like eleven or twelve, but I haven't been home lately."

"Surely you don't keep them all in the house?"

"Only a few at a time on a rotating basis. I try to give equal time to each one."

"Just like a harem," Stephanie remarked lightly. "It's a good thing you collect dogs instead of wives. The jealousy factor would be a problem."

"I never could understand why any man would want a harem. One wife is enough—when she's the right one." His enigmatic eyes roamed over her face.

"Brave talk from a single man," Stephanie scoffed. "You probably have a harem already, without any of the responsibilities."

"Do you really believe that?"

"Do you expect me to believe you're celibate?" she countered.

"No, I'm a normal, healthy male. But I've never been promiscuous."

"I suppose you can't afford to be, in your position."

"The hell with my position!" he exclaimed angrily. "You keep using that as a shield between us. I'm the same man I was when we met."

"Not really, but it doesn't matter. Fortunately we didn't . . . get involved." She looked away from his penetrating gaze.

"But that wasn't the reason. Why wouldn't you let me make love to you, Stephanie?" he asked intently.

"I don't indulge in casual affairs," she answered, still without looking at him.

"You considered our relationship a brief encounter?"

"What else would you call it? We had fun together, but we both knew it would be over when the week ended."

"And that was all right with you?"

He mustn't know how she'd longed for some sign that this wasn't simply a vacation romance. That was before she knew they had no future together, of course. In attempting to salvage her pride she went too far.

"One often meets a charming man on vacation," she said carelessly.

"Does one?" His expression was mocking. "And does one also tremble in his arms and call out his name over and over again when he touches her?"

"Morgan, please." She stared down at her twisting fingers.

He jerked her chin up to make her look at him. "Please what? Please don't remind you of how much you wanted me? If we hadn't been interrupted that night we would have made love. Can you deny that?"

"No," she murmured, since they both knew the answer.

"Do you usually respond that way to all the charming men you meet on vacation?"

"You're very experienced," she answered haltingly. " got carried away."

"Not completely," he replied sardonically.

"There has to be more," she whispered.

"You don't feel anything for me but desire?" he asked in a flat tone of voice.

Why was he tormenting her like this? Did his ego demand that every woman fall in love with him? She was tempted to tell him the truth and put an end to the agony. Her nails made crescent marks in her palms as she struggled for control.

"What difference does it make?" she asked hopelessly. "After tonight we'll never see each other again."

Stephanie had succeeded in masking her yearning, but not before Morgan caught a glimpse of it. His eyes glittered as he looked at her lowered head. "Then I guess we'd better make this a special night."

She stiffened warily at his dulcet tone. "It already has been."

"Not like it could be."

She stood up quickly, spilling the brochure on the floor. "I think it's time we went to dinner."

He stood up, too. "Are you afraid of me, Stephanie?"

"No, of course not! I just . . . it's getting late."

When she would have moved away, his hands clasped her waist and turned her to face him. "We have all night."

Her body tensed. "Let go of me, Morgan."

"That isn't what you really want." He smiled meltingly.

She sucked in her breath sharply. "I can't believe you would—"

"Would what, my love?" The pressure of his hands increased, drawing her gently toward him.

Her own hands went up defensively to splay against his chest. "Why are you doing this?" she pleaded. "You could have almost any woman you wanted. You don't have to use force."

"I don't intend to." His mouth slid down her cheek.

She jerked her head away. "What do you call this?"

His chuckle had a deep male sound. "Friendly persuasion."

"I don't think that's—" She turned her head and the indignant words died as her lips brushed his.

"That's your problem," he murmured. "You think too much. You need to relax and enjoy."

Each statement was punctuated by a tiny kiss that left her wanting more. As she tried to fight the desire, he folded her in his arms. The contact with his lean body was enflaming enough, but he heightened the sensation by trailing his fingers up and down her spine. Her gown was cut almost to the waist in back, and his caresses on her bare skin were extremely erotic.

The assault on her senses was irresistible. All the reasons this was wrong were buried under an avalanche of longing. She ached to feel their bodies entwined, had a burning need to experience his full possession. With a sigh of surrender she wound her arms around his neck and lifted her face for his kiss.

Morgan reacted with joy. His mouth closed over hers convulsively and his tongue plunged deeply. Their bodies were taut as they strained against each other, both gripped by ever mounting passion.

When he finally dragged his mouth away, Stephanie was trembling. "We've wasted so much time," she whispered, rubbing her cheek against his. "I wish you'd brought me here sooner."

The urgency drained out of Morgan's face, leaving his expression bleak. His fingers closed over hers as she reached up to untie his tie.

Stephanie sensed the change and lifted her head to look up at him. "What's wrong, Morgan?"

He put her gently away. "I'm sorry, Stephanie."

"I don't understand," she said uncertainly. "Don't you want to make love to me?"

He groaned and reached for her, then let his arms drop. "More than anything in the world, but not through trickery."

"What do you mean?"

He took both her hands and held them tightly. "I told you I would never seduce you, yet that's exactly what I've done tonight. You're so vulnerable, sweetheart. I want you more than you'll ever know, but I can't take you this way. You have to come to me freely, or not at all."

She withdrew her hands in order to make a clear-headed decision. Morgan was right in one way. He was powerfully seductive. As she gazed at the man she loved, Stephanie knew she didn't have a choice. Taking the coward's way out would mean regrets for the rest of her life.

"Maybe I wasn't sure at first, but I know this is what I want," she said steadily.

Something flared in his eyes. "Without commitment?"

She nodded.

His embrace was almost painful, but after his initial reaction Morgan's caresses were gentle. He kissed her eyelids and the corner of her mouth, murmuring tender words of affection.

Once her decision was made, Stephanie allowed herself all the pleasures that were forbidden before. She traced his high cheekbones and the curve of his generous mouth, kissed the hollow at the base of his throat and slipped her hand inside his shirt to touch his flat nipples.

His hand closed around her questing fingers. "Sweet Stephanie, you're driving me wild," he gasped.

"I've wanted to touch you for such a long time."

"Before this night is over we'll know everything about each other," he promised in a hoarse voice.

The zipper at her waist yielded to his manipulation. With a little nudge to her shoulder straps, the gown slid over her hips and settled in a silken heap on the floor. Stephanie was left only in sheer panty hose. She shivered slightly, but not from the cold—just the opposite. Morgan's burning gaze was wrapping her in warmth.

He reached out and touched her breasts. After feathering them with his fingertips he cupped their fullness in his palms and circled each rosy tip with his thumb.

"So beautiful," he murmured. "Your skin is like warm alabaster."

His mouth enveloped one bud, lapping it with his tongue until she cried out with delight and dug her fingers into the hard muscles of his shoulders as he knelt before her. She needed the support when he trailed a line of kisses down her flat midriff, pausing to roll her panty hose down her hips. Molten excitement gripped her as he followed the filmy garment with his lips.

He looked up with incandescent eyes when she drew in her breath sharply. "Give in to it, darling. I want this night to be special."

She sank down beside him and put her arms around his neck. "Then love me, Morgan, please love me."

Stephanie knew the literal part of her plea was futile, but it didn't matter. For this one night he would belong to her.

He lifted her in his arms and carried her over to the bed. While his mouth covered hers she unbuttoned his shirt. He shrugged it off and bent over her, moving in a slow rhythm so their bodies barely grazed each other. The tips of her breasts were so sensitized that she shuddered with pleasure at the tantalizing contact.

Her fingers fumbled with eagerness as she unfastened his belt. He took over for her and removed the rest of his clothing with an urgency that matched hers. When their nude bodies touched, a flame leaped between them.

"I didn't know it was possible to want anyone this much," he muttered.

"I never have," she whispered.

He paused above her for what seemed like an endless moment, staring down at her passion-filled face with tawny eyes. "You're mine now, and I'll never let you go."

When she held out her arms he clasped her tightly, uniting their bodies with a deep thrust that intensified her hunger. She moved against him in a frenzied struggle for release from the throbbing torment that was escalating out of control.

Their bodies strained against each other, joined by a burning bond that fused them together. Each plateau brought greater sensation, until they reached the summit and found ecstasy. She clung to him as powerful spasms racked her. They diminished gradually, leaving her spent but totally fulfilled.

She was quiet in his arms afterward, too content to move a muscle. When Morgan finally stirred and stroked her hair some time later, Stephanie felt like purring.

"Any regrets?" he asked unexpectedly.

She opened her eyes. "Not a one. I never even knew it could be like this."

"Why did you change your mind?" The tone of his voice surprised her as much as the question. He sounded so serious.

"I hope you're not sorry I did," she joked.

"You know better than that. But you didn't answer me."

She smiled. "Do you want to hear how irresistible you are?"

"I want the truth. Why did you let me make love to you tonight?"

Some of her euphoria diminished. "What difference does it make?"

"A great deal." He levered himself up on one elbow to look down at her intently. "You assured me that I wasn't seducing you."

Her tension drained away. "Is that what's bothering you?" She smoothed his ruffled hair. "You can stop worrying. I knew exactly what I was doing."

"I'm glad of that, but it doesn't tell me what I need to know."

"You're being rather... insensitive."

"I'm sorry. I don't mean to be, but it's important."

She drew away from him and pulled the sheet up to cover her nakedness. "Why are you doing this, Morgan? A few minutes ago we . . ." Her long lashes drooped.

He cupped her cheek tenderly. "We were good together, weren't we?"

"I'll never forget tonight," she answered simply.

"Because you slept with a king?"

She felt as though he'd dumped a bucket of freezing water over her. "How could you say such a thing?" she gasped.

He steeled himself against her hurt. "What else can I think? You weren't willing before."

"That's not—I wanted—" She stopped to compose herself. It was unthinkable for him to believe such a degrading thing. But it was equally insupportable for him to discover the truth.

"I know you're attracted to me," he said patiently. "I'm trying to find out if my allure is merely physical."

She gave him a startled look. Had she betrayed herself in some way? "Does it really matter?" she asked warily.

"Yes, a great deal in your case." He sighed. "I've never cared before. I've come to terms with the fact that a certain amount of glamour is attached to . . . having a relationship with someone like me," he finished delicately.

Blind anger swept through Stephanie. She'd given herself without reservation, and he was cheapening her gift!

"Do you expect sympathy from me? It's all right when you take advantage of women, but when the shoe is on the other foot it's quite another thing, is that it?" she flared. "Well, I don't happen to be one of your groupies. I fell in love with you before I ever knew you were a king!"

Excitement blazed on his face. "That's what I had to know."

Stephanie was appalled at how anger had betrayed her. She started to scramble out of bed, intent only on hiding her shame. But Morgan pulled her back into his arms.

"Let go of me," she panted. "You've gotten everything you want."

He subdued her easily. "I'll never get enough of you."

"If you think for one minute that I'd ever let you touch me again, you're badly mistaken," she raged. "You are the most unfeeling, conceited, arrogant—"

He cut off her furious words by pressing her against the pillow and covering her mouth with his. She intensified her struggles, but Morgan gathered her close and wound his legs around hers.

She was powerless in his arms, as defenseless against him physically as she was in every other way. The hopelessness of the situation took all the fight out of her.

When she became passive in his arms Morgan raised his head. "That's better. Are you ready to talk reasonably now?"

"We've both said enough already."

He smiled. "It wasn't easy getting the truth out of you."

Her eyes flashed green fire. "I didn't know you had such a monumental ego."

"If I had, I wouldn't have been so insecure with you. Would you really have walked out of my life without a backward glance?"

"Neither of us has any obligation to the other."

"That was before love reared its lovely head."

"You needn't worry about me. I'll get over it," she promised grimly.

"I hope not." He kissed the tip of her nose. "At least not for forty or fifty years. That's how long I expect our honeymoon to last."

Her anger was sidetracked momentarily. "What are you talking about?"

"I'm asking you to marry me."

She searched his face for signs of mockery, but Morgan seemed to be in earnest. "I can't believe you really mean it," she said nonetheless.

"What can I do to convince you? I love you," he said quietly. "I want to spend the rest of my life making you happy."

"But that's impossible!"

"Why? You said you love me, too."

"That has nothing to do with it. You can't marry someone like me."

"I never thought I'd be this fortunate." He kissed her with great tenderness.

She turned her head. "Morgan, you mustn't. I can't think when you do that."

He chuckled. "That's the general idea. We get into all kinds of trouble when you use your head instead of your heart."

She looked back at him then, experiencing a rush of love so great it was almost an ache. But cold reality couldn't be ignored. "One of us has to use common sense, and you obviously aren't thinking clearly. You're a king. You have to marry someone from your own world."

His eyes twinkled mischievously. "I'll admit you're utterly unique, but you're still part of this world."

"Not yours, though. I don't know anything about protocol or international politics, not to mention royalty. I wouldn't fit into your life."

"You did very nicely tonight. I overheard glowing compliments about you."

"That's very gratifying, but this was simply a social event."

"You held your own with a group of intelligent and powerful people." He gazed at her fondly. "You don't realize how much you have to offer, but you will in time. You're going to make a magnificent queen."

The prospect was daunting. "What about your people?" she asked desperately. "They'd never accept me."

"They'll love you almost as much as I do—which is saying a great deal," he murmured, stroking her bare body with awakening desire.

The temptation to accept this gift from above was almost overwhelming, but Stephanie was afraid she'd wind up living in the opposite place from heaven. Morgan was too blinded by passion to realize that every one of her objections was valid. She couldn't bear to see his disillusion when they came true.

Reaching out to still his hand, she said, "Has it ever occurred to you that if we'd made love at the beginning of the week, you might not be as anxious to make a commitment now?"

He stared at her incredulously. "You can't really believe I'm being carried away by the moment. I'm hardly a schoolboy, entranced by his first sexual experience. Don't you realize that I want so much more from you? I want to be with you through the good times and the bad, to have children with you and share our lives. If you really loved me you'd want that, too."

"Oh, Morgan, I do! I just want you to be sure."

His intense expression changed to tenderness. "I think I knew the first moment I saw you."

His kiss was deeply reassuring. Stephanie was filled with such blinding happiness that her doubts were swept away. Miracles did happen!

When he finally dragged his mouth from hers, Morgan said, "I wish we didn't have to go to London. I'd like to take you straight to Verlaine, but it can't be helped."

Stephanie stirred in his arms. "I have to go home tomorrow, Morgan."

"You can put the girls on the plane by themselves. They're not babies."

"I'm still responsible for them. Besides, I have a job. I can't walk out without notice."

He frowned. "You can carry a sense of responsibility too far. We have our own plans to make."

"There isn't any hurry," she said hesitantly.

"It's nice to know where your priorities lie." His tone was frosty.

"Be reasonable, Morgan. This was all so unexpected. I need time to make arrangements."

"Is planning a wedding on your agenda? Whether we like it or not, it has to be a full-scale event—hundreds of guests, days of festivities, television coverage." Her open dismay softened his austerity. "Don't worry, darling, I'll take care of the details. You won't have to do much more than select your wedding gown and give me a guest list."

"Everything will take a lot of time, won't it?"

"Unfortunately." He sighed.

"Then it won't matter if I go home tomorrow."

"It will matter a great deal to *me*. I want you with me."

"You'll be terribly busy, and I have things to do, too. I have to tell my sister, put all my business affairs in order, pack up my personal things." She looked daunted at the enormity of the job facing her.

"I know this is a big step for you," he said gently. "I'm asking you to leave your country and move to a place you've never even seen. But I promise to make you happy. Just don't stop loving me."

"I never could." She put her arms around his neck and lifted her face.

Morgan's possession was even more thrilling this time because it was a beginning, not an ending. They were joined spiritually as well as physically at the magic moment of fulfillment.

Stephanie wanted to lie in his arms forever, savoring the peace that was the aftermath of love. But when she heard the muffled chimes of a grandfather clock in the hall she stirred reluctantly.

"It's terribly late, Morgan. I have to go."

"I know, but I wish you didn't." His sigh mingled with hers. "I resent having to share you with anyone."

"Cindy and Bambi are scarcely competition," she teased.

"No, they're allies." He grinned. "I'd like to see their faces when they hear the news."

Stephanie paused with one leg out of bed. "I'm not going to tell them. Good Lord, it would be all over school in a flash!"

"You have some objection to people knowing we're engaged?" he asked evenly.

"No, of course not, but you don't know what sixteen-year-old girls are like. That's all they'd want to talk about. I wouldn't be able to teach them a thing."

"I thought you were going back to resign."

"Well, yes, but not right away. I mean, I won't be leaving immediately."

He gazed at her enigmatically for a long moment. "If you're getting cold feet, this is the time to say so. I'd rather see it end now than have you decide later that you don't want to marry me."

Her blood chilled at the thought of losing Morgan. She'd been resigned to giving him up before, but not now.

"I haven't changed my mind," she said hurriedly. "I guess I'm just . . . scared. I've seen royal weddings on television. They were spectacles!"

He pulled her back into his arms. "That part will be over with before you know it, and then we'll have the rest of our lives together."

"Give me a little time to get used to the idea," she pleaded. "After the news gets out I won't have any privacy."

"I couldn't sympathize with you more, but we have to announce our engagement. I can't simply spring it on my people at the last minute."

"I'm only asking for a few weeks," she coaxed. "You have your conference to attend first, anyway."

Morgan was clearly unhappy about the situation, but he finally gave in. "All right, you win. I can see who's going to run the country," he said fondly. "I'll give you one month, and then I'm going to tell the whole world you belong to me. Is that clear?"

It was almost morning by the time Stephanie got to bed, but sleep was impossible. Elation and apprehension warred inside her. Would Morgan's ardor cool when he was back in his own element? Would he begin to wonder if he'd made a terrible mistake?

That was the main reason she'd requested a grace period before publicizing their engagement. It would be a crushing blow if her fears were correct, but not as devastating as being trapped in a loveless marriage.

No matter what happened, though, nothing would ever dim the perfection of this night. She smiled and closed her eyes to relive every stirring moment.

Chapter Six

Morgan drove Stephanie and her wards to the airport the next day and solidified his standing with Cindy and Bambi by buying them magazines, candy and last-minute souvenirs.

"You're really neat, Mr. Destine." Cindy's admiration changed to uncertainty. "Or am I supposed to call you Your Highness?"

"I'd rather you didn't." He smiled.

"I still can't get over it." Bambi stared appraisingly at his tight jeans and chest-hugging shirt. "No one would ever know you're a king."

"I assure you I'm like any other man in all the ways that count." His amused glance at Stephanie made her color rise.

"You won't forget to send us a picture, will you?" Cindy reminded him.

"As soon as I get home," he promised. "They'll be boarding your plane any minute now, so why don't you girls get in line?"

"They want to be alone," Bambi told Cindy in a loud whisper.

Morgan linked his arms around Stephanie's shoulders and gazed at her affectionately. "Parting isn't sweet sorrow, it's hell. How can I get along without you for a month?"

"It won't be easy for me, either," she murmured.

"Then come to me sooner," he urged. "You can get everything done in a week."

She was greatly tempted, but the stakes were too high. "I couldn't possibly, but just think how glad you'll be to see me when I do get there," she answered lightly.

"Does this give you some idea?" He took her in his arms and kissed her with passion and tenderness, oblivious of the people around them.

Stephanie was still floating on a cloud of happiness when she boarded the plane and took her seat.

The girls smugly surveyed her dazzled face. "Do you still expect us to believe you and Mr. Destine are only friends?" Cindy asked.

"I never had a friend kiss *me* that way," Bambi commented.

Stephanie pulled herself together hastily. "I hope you get these romantic notions out of your head before we get home," she said crisply. "Mr. Destine would be as annoyed as I if you spread rumors about us. In fact, it would be a good idea if you didn't mention him at all."

"Not tell the kids we met a king?" Bambi asked indignantly.

Stephanie realized that was too much to expect. "Well, at least leave me out of it," she warned.

* * *

Classes resumed at Miss Waycroft's, and things were so normal that sometimes Stephanie thought the week in Florida was only a dream. Morgan's nightly phone calls made the dream come alive, but they were too brief, and her contact with him was too tenuous.

"Will you send me a picture, too, when you get home?" she asked forlornly one night. "I don't have anything to remember you by."

"I don't need anything to help me remember *you*," he answered in a smoky voice. "When I close my eyes I can see every curve of your delicious body."

The next day she received a picture by express mail. It was a studio portrait of a regal monarch, not the warm, laughing man she knew, but Stephanie treasured it. Across the bottom of the photo he'd written in a bold hand: "To my future queen. All my love, Morgan."

She bought a frame and put it on her bedside table where his beloved face would be the first thing she saw in the morning, and the last thing at night.

After a short time Morgan left for London. Two days went by without his usual phone calls. He was apologetic when he called on the third night.

"I'm sorry, darling." He sounded very far away. "What with all the briefing sessions and the constant receptions, I haven't had a minute to call you."

"That's all right," she answered as a cold chill rippled up her spine. This was what she expected.

"It *isn't* all right," he complained. "When I *have* had a chance to phone, it was the middle of the night back there. You don't know how frustrating it's been to picture you all curled up in bed."

"I thought your conference was supposed to be business," she remarked in a small voice. "It sounds as though it's mostly social."

"That's where a lot of alliances are formed. You have to play the game." His voice was vibrant. Morgan was clearly enjoying himself.

"Well, I'm glad you're having a good time." She tried to sound sincere.

"How can I without you? I miss you, angel," he said deeply.

"I miss you, too," she whispered.

The next two weeks were disturbing. Stephanie had vivid images of Morgan surrounded by admiring women eager to do anything to capture his attention. He professed distaste for that kind of adulation, but he was a very virile man. And there were many beautiful and clever women in his world.

Stephanie tried desperately to hang on to her trust. She forced herself to make allowances for the constant round of festivities, accepting his assurance that they were necessary. Her only hope was that things would change when he returned to Verlaine.

His first call from there wasn't reassuring, however. They hadn't spoken in two days, and she was hoping for fevered protestations of love and longing. Instead, Morgan sounded very formal.

"I'm sorry I couldn't get back to you sooner," he said, as though talking to a business associate. "I've run into a number of problems at this end."

"That's quite all right. I understand," she replied stiffly.

"It has nothing to do with . . . the matter pending between us."

"Don't worry about it," she answered airily, not believing him for a moment, but intent on salvaging her pride.

"I knew I could count on you." His voice warmed.

Stephanie hung up with a feeling of doom. Morgan hadn't told her he loved her, or even that he missed her.

The days dragged on without getting any better. Morgan seemed to be slipping farther and farther away from her, sounding more remote on the telephone each time he called. The one thing she had to be grateful for was that no one knew the plans they'd made when a tropic moon wove its romantic spell. She hadn't resigned her position, nor told her sister. After she released Morgan from his commitment, life would go on without anyone the wiser.

All that changed when Bambi discovered Morgan's photograph. Stephanie had asked the young girl to pick up some test papers she'd neglected to bring to class. In all fairness, the photo was there for anyone to see; Stephanie had simply forgotten about it. Bambi had been rebuffed about Morgan too often to comment on the inscription he'd penned, but she shared her information with the rest of the student body.

The first warning Stephanie had was when a reporter from the local newspaper called her, wanting to know if it was true that she was going to marry the King of Verlaine. After her initial shock, she parried the question and demanded to know the source of his information, but the reporter wouldn't reveal it. Stephanie had a fairly shrewd idea, however.

She called Bambi and Cindy into her office and confronted them. "Did you tell the *Clarion* that I was going to marry Mr. Destine?"

Cindy indignantly disclaimed any responsibility, but Bambi looked guilty. "I didn't think Debra would tell her father," she said defensively. Debra Potter's father was editor of the *Clarion*.

"How could you make up such a story?" Stephanie exclaimed.

"Maybe I shouldn't have told anyone, but how could it be a secret when Mr. Destine said right on his picture that you were his future queen?"

"You weren't supposed to—I mean, it was just a joke." Stephanie tried to sound convincing.

"Signing it 'all my love always' sounds pretty serious to me," Bambi replied stubbornly.

"You don't understand. You never have." Stephanie mastered her agitation with an effort. "Well, I suppose it doesn't matter. The *Clarion* is only a small-town newspaper. I want this gossip stopped immediately, though. Is that crystal clear?"

She thought that was the end of it until she received a long-distance call from the *Boston Globe*. It was followed by other calls from major newspapers around the country. They all wanted confirmation of her upcoming marriage. Stephanie flatly denied any involvement with Morgan, but they scented a story and pursued it like vultures. Then one evening when she was watching the news on television, her house of cards came tumbling down.

"And now for a happier note in international news," the anchorman said. "That rumor about a royal wedding has been confirmed by the King of Verlaine. He announced today that he plans to marry Stephanie Blair, an American schoolteacher."

Stephanie didn't hear any more. She stared at the television screen in shock as the picture shifted after a few moments to warfare in a distant land. How had the story spread so fast, and why had Morgan confirmed it? Out of a sense of chivalry, no doubt. He thought she'd given out the news, and he felt honor bound to back her up. She had to get in touch with him immediately.

Calling Verlaine long distance wasn't easy, especially since she didn't know Morgan's number. When she finally reached the palace more confusion ensued. She never did get to talk to him, but she left an urgent message. By the time he called back she was a nervous wreck, although less than an hour had elapsed.

"I just got your message," he said. "I suppose the press have been hounding you, but you must have known it was inevitable once you talked to even one reporter."

"But I didn't!"

"Then how did they find out? When the wire services contacted me, I naturally assumed you must have given them the story."

"No! It was all a mistake. Bambi saw your picture and—well, it doesn't matter. Reporters have been calling me, but I told them none of it is true. You can tell them you simply misunderstood their questions."

"Why would I do that? I was thrilled to be able to make our engagement public. It's what I've wanted all along."

"You don't have to keep up the pretense, Morgan," she said forlornly. "I know you don't want to marry me."

After a stunned silence he said, "What's gotten into you? I've been crossing off the days until we can be together."

"You didn't sound like you missed me," she said in a small voice. "You've been so formal on the phone."

"That was *your* fault! You made me promise not to tell anyone, and just lately I always seem to be surrounded by people. I had to talk to you no matter what, but I couldn't say the things I wanted to."

The ice around Stephanie's heart melted. "You weren't regretting your proposal?"

"Do you remember the night we made love, and the things I said to you?" His voice was husky with emotion. "I mean them even more now than I did then."

"Oh, Morgan, I love you so," she whispered.

"Then come to me, darling," he urged. "There's no reason to wait now."

Practical matters intruded, and she had to make a reluctant confession. "I haven't handed in my resignation yet."

"What?"

"I wanted to give you time to change your mind—and I thought you had."

Morgan was having trouble controlling himself. Finally he said, "You have till the end of the month. If you're not here by then I'm coming to get you!"

Miss Cunningham, the headmistress, was very understanding when Stephanie talked to her the next morning.

"It's all terribly romantic. I'm so happy for you, my dear, although we'll be sorry to lose you, of course."

"I'll miss you and the girls, too."

The older woman smiled. "I doubt that. You'll be leading a very glamorous life."

"I suppose so. It's a little frightening to contemplate."

"Nonsense. You're a Waycroft girl," Miss Cunningham said stoutly. "You'll be a credit to us, and a real inspiration to your students. We'll have a gala going-away party at the end of the term."

"I don't think you understand," Stephanie said carefully. "I'll stay until you find a replacement, naturally, but I'd like to leave as soon as possible."

"In the middle of the school year?" The headmistress looked like a ruffled chicken. "That would be quite upsetting."

Morgan would be a lot *more* upset at any further post-ponements. "My fiancé is most anxious to have me join him," Stephanie answered tentatively.

"I'm sure he'd want you to honor your obligations."

Stephanie felt caught between a rock and a hard place. "You will try to find someone, won't you?" she asked hopelessly.

The solution to her problem came from an unexpected source. As soon as Morgan confirmed their engagement, the media descended on Miss Waycroft's in full force. Reporters were augmented by photographers who snapped pictures of everything and everybody.

They even invaded the school, trying to get photos of Stephanie in her classroom. When the headmistress sternly evicted them they camped outside, interviewing anyone who ventured out the door. The girls loved it. Even the ones who'd never taken a class from Stephanie basked in the spotlight.

Finally Miss Cunningham threw in the towel. She called Stephanie into her office and suggested that she leave immediately.

From the air, Verlaine looked like a magic kingdom. Gentle hills enclosed a small city that sparkled like a jewel in the late afternoon sunshine. As her plane circled lower for a landing, Stephanie could see that the lush green areas were parks filled with riotous flowers.

Her heart was pounding with anticipation as the wheels touched down. The long weeks of waiting were over. In a few minutes she'd be in Morgan's arms.

Their reunion was much different than she'd imagined, however. As she emerged from the plane a small army of photographers began snapping pictures. A little girl at the foot of the steps presented her with a huge bouquet of red roses, and a distinguished older man welcomed her to the country.

Stephanie responded automatically, but her heart wasn't in it. Where was Morgan? Then she saw him standing a short distance away. After the formalities were over he came forward and kissed her hand. His expression was remote, but the pressure of his fingers told her what she needed to know.

"I'm very happy that you're here," he said formally, then added for her ears alone, "finally!"

Her smile held a hint of mischief at his frustration. "It's a great pleasure for me, too," she answered demurely.

Morgan introduced her briefly to several dignitaries before leading her to a long black limousine. His aide held open the door.

"You two haven't met formally, but I'm sure you remember Jacques," Morgan said wryly as the young man got into the car with them.

"I feel as though I know him well," Stephanie answered with a hint of laughter.

"I hope you'll be more forgiving than Phillipe," Jacques answered. "He threatened to fire me every day of that week in Florida."

"He knew you were only doing your job." She turned to Morgan. "Will I have to call you Phillipe?"

"Darling will suffice." His tone was joking, but something flared momentarily in his eyes.

They were sitting well separated from each other on the wide seat, yet his leashed desire was almost tangible. It was met and matched by her own. The urge to reach out and touch him was almost irresistible.

Their behavior was necessarily circumspect, however. As the car traveled through the city they made polite conversation while Jacques indicated points of interest.

Ravenna Castle looked exactly as it had in the photograph, a huge stone building with towers and turrets, set in the middle of parklike grounds. It was perhaps the most romantic thing Stephanie had ever seen, conjuring up images of knights in armor jousting on spirited horses. She could only stare speechlessly.

"Welcome home," Morgan said softly.

She turned to him with shining eyes. "Oh, Morgan, it's magnificent."

"I'd hoped you'd think so."

The baronial front door was opened by an older man in livery, whom Morgan introduced as Maurice, the major-domo. Behind him was a line of servants waiting to greet her. Morgan introduced them, also, impressing Stephanie with his ability to remember all their names. She only hoped *she* would. It evidently took a lot of help to run a castle.

When the servants had gone, Stephanie looked around at the rooms branching off the great hall. "I want to see everything."

"Later." Morgan took her hand and hustled her up one side of the double staircase that curved gracefully to the second floor. "You must be tired from your trip. I'll show you to your room."

She barely got a glimpse of it. As soon as they were inside with the door closed, he took her in his arms and kissed her with all the pent-up yearning their separation had brought. His deep hunger was evident in the kisses he strewed over her face and neck while he caressed her body in a frenzy of renewed discovery.

"God, how I've missed you," he growled. "I thought you'd never get here."

"I had doubts myself for a while," she answered soberly.

"How *could* you?"

"I won't ever have again." It was a promise Stephanie intended to keep. Nothing would shake her confidence in Morgan.

His kiss this time was sweetly reassuring, a reaffirmation of their love. But when the familiar tides of passion started to rise between them he reluctantly dragged his mouth away.

"A little more of this and I'll take you to bed and keep you there for a week," he said.

"I wouldn't mind," she murmured.

"Don't make it more difficult," he groaned. "My brother and sister-in-law are waiting to meet you, and I'm sure you want to inspect your new home."

Stephanie could have postponed both events, but she didn't say so. "Was your family surprised at the news about us?"

Morgan's mouth curved derisively. "That's putting it mildly. For once in her life Lydia was speechless—for about a minute and a half, anyway."

"They weren't pleased?" Stephanie faltered.

"They don't have anything to say about it." His chilled expression gave her a glimpse of how autocratic Morgan could be when he was displeased.

"I was hoping they'd like me."

"They'll adore you. How could anyone help it?" When she continued to look dubious he took her in his arms. "Trust me, angel. Nothing and nobody will ever come between us."

"I realize it's probably because I'm an untitled American, but I just wish they'd reserved judgment until we met."

"Don't take it personally. Lydia wouldn't approve of anyone I married. I've always known that."

"Why not?"

"It's quite simple. As long as I remain a bachelor, she continues to act as my hostess at official affairs. Lydia enjoys her position as the highest-ranking female member of the monarchy. Once I'm married she'll naturally have to step aside."

"But surely she knew you'd marry someday."

"I haven't shown any inclination until now." He grinned.

Stephanie looked at him and shook her head. Morgan was not only dashingly handsome, he was virile and charismatic as well. "With so many beautiful women in the world, it's hard to believe you've stayed single so long."

"I was waiting for you, my love. There couldn't be anyone else for me."

"Or me," she answered softly. "Maybe when Lydia sees that, she won't resent me as much."

Morgan's tender expression hardened. "I wouldn't worry about it if I were you." He dismissed the entire subject. "This will be your suite. You can redecorate it any way you please."

Stephanie looked around for the first time and discovered an opulent apartment. The sitting room was furnished with graceful chairs and a sofa covered with rose-colored damask that matched the looped-back draperies at the tall windows. A magnificent pale blue Oriental rug covered the floor, and an antique writing desk was placed between the windows.

"You might want a different color scheme, or perhaps a more modern feeling," Morgan commented.

"Oh, no, I wouldn't change a single thing!"

"Well, you don't have to decide right now. Take a look at the bedroom and bath."

The bedroom was as large as the sitting room, and decorated in the same color scheme of subtle pinks and blues. A four-poster bed at one end was covered with a quilted velvet spread in a muted shade of old rose, and the china shepherdess lamps on each side of the bed had pale blue shades.

The bathroom was perhaps more incredible. It had a sunken tub in the middle of the floor with faucets of rose quartz in the shape of fans. There was also a glass-enclosed shower in one corner of the spacious room. The walls and floor were all done in marble, except for one long wall that was completely mirrored.

"I never expected anything like this," Stephanie exclaimed.

"The baths have all been modernized," Morgan explained. "Your dressing room is over here."

He led the way to a separate room with hanging space for hundreds of garments. Shelves and chests of drawers were built in along one entire wall to accommodate lingerie, shoes and accessories. Everything was empty, awaiting her meager wardrobe.

As they walked back to the bedroom Stephanie was puzzling over a disturbing thought. Morgan said this was *her* bedroom, *her* bath. Didn't he intend to share it with her?

"Does it meet with your approval?" he asked.

"Everything is beautiful," she answered politely.

"But?" He was alerted by her noncommittal tone. "Tell me. If anything displeases you we'll change it."

"It isn't that. I was just wondering... will I be staying here after we're married?"

He didn't seem to understand. "Don't married people usually live together?"

"That's what I always thought," she murmured.

He led her over to the bed, sat her down and took the place beside her. "What's this all about, Stephanie? Any problems we have can be worked out if we talk about them."

After a moment's hesitation she said, "I realize our customs are different, but in my country married couples sleep... I mean they share..." She stumbled to a halt.

Relief chased away his concern. "Did you honestly think we were going to sleep in separate rooms?"

"You said all of this was mine. You didn't say ours."

"Darling little Stephanie, how could you think I'd choose to sleep alone if you were anywhere in the vicinity? Your problem will be escaping from my bed." The banked fires in his eyes began to glow as he urged her gently onto her back and bent over to kiss the hollow in her throat.

His ardor left no doubt, yet she was still confused. "You mean you're going to sleep in here with me?"

"If that's your choice, although I'd prefer my room. I've dreamed of making love to you there for so long."

"Then why do we have separate rooms?"

"These are your private quarters where you can entertain friends informally and take care of your personal affairs. Or simply steal away by yourself and read if you feel like it. The bedroom just happens to be part of the apartment." He grinned suddenly. "Perhaps some distant queens slept in this bed alone, but I doubt it. My hot blood has to have been inherited from my ancestors."

"You can understand my confusion when I started getting mixed signals," she explained, feeling slightly foolish.

"I'll clear up any lingering doubts."

He unbuttoned the top buttons of her blouse and kissed the valley between her breasts while he trailed a finger along the top of her lacy bra. Any residual strangeness Stephanie had felt at her surroundings vanished. It didn't matter where they were. This was the man she'd fallen in love with, the one she wanted to live with for the rest of her life.

When Morgan's tongue found one rosy peak through the concealing lace, she drew in her breath. He caressed both swelling mounds until she uttered a low moan of desire.

"I thought I must have imagined the perfection of your body." He opened her blouse to the waist and unclasped her bra. "I told myself no woman could be this exquisite, but you are."

Her skin was still golden from the sun, except for one pale strip that her bikini top had covered. He traced the dividing line sensuously, then bent his head to follow the path with his lips.

A simmering warmth spread through her. She wrapped her arms tightly around his torso and pulled him down on top of her. His weight crushed her into the soft bed, but she strained even closer, wanting to feel the full strength of his muscular body.

After a feverish moment he rolled away. "It's been so long, my love." His voice was hoarse. "I don't know if I can wait any longer."

"I don't want you to," she breathed.

Their clothing fluttered to the floor like autumn leaves as they undressed each other in a frenzied rush. Morgan's body was a torch, igniting embers of desire into flames of passion.

Their coupling was as turbulent as a storm at sea. They rode wave after wave of sensation until a last giant swell tossed them into quieter waters. Clinging together afterward, they were awed by the intensity of their feeling.

Morgan finally rolled onto his side, taking her with him. "I trust that answers all your questions about our living arrangements."

"Most satisfactorily." She smiled. "I hope we have more misunderstandings."

"That won't be necessary." His expression was suddenly serious. "Promise you'll come to me if you're troubled by anything."

"I promise," she agreed readily.

"A lot of things will seem strange to you in these first weeks," he said slowly. "Just remember that I'm always here for you."

Her heart swelled with love. "You don't have to worry about me. I'll even win over Lydia."

Morgan sighed. "They're undoubtedly waiting to meet you."

"They live here in the castle, don't they?"

"Yes, but in a separate wing. You needn't be concerned that they'll be underfoot."

"I'm not," she replied, although she was, slightly.

Lydia was an unknown quantity. Things could get a bit sticky if she proved difficult. But Stephanie wasn't really worried. She and Morgan loved each other. Nothing Lydia or anyone else could do would ever change that.

Morgan got out of bed, magnificent to her eyes in his nudity. "I'll have your luggage sent up so you can change," he said.

"I'd appreciate that." She looked up at him through long lashes. "I don't suppose you'd like to bathe with me in that wonderful tub?"

He leaned down and kissed her. "One of your better ideas. I'll tell Henri we'll see them tomorrow."

"No, you'd better not," she said reluctantly. "I don't want to start off by hurting their feelings. I'll take a shower instead. It will be quicker."

Morgan grinned. "Especially if you take it alone."

Stephanie had braced herself for hostility, but Henri and Lydia couldn't have been more charming. Henri resembled his brother, yet he lacked Morgan's dynamism. He was more laid back, as though life was a big joke that was meant to be enjoyed but not taken seriously.

Lydia seemed the stronger of the two. She was a tall, cool blonde, with a more regal bearing than her husband. Her rather thin lips and square jaw gave the impression that she could be quite autocratic, but Lydia was making every effort to be friendly now.

"We've been so anxious to meet the woman who finally captured our king," she said to Stephanie.

"I feel like a chess piece," Morgan remarked dryly.

"I've been looking forward to meeting you, too," Stephanie responded, ignoring his comment. "I hope we'll be friends as well as relatives."

"I know we will be," Lydia answered warmly. "I hope you'll call on me if there is anything I can do to make your life smoother."

"That's very kind of you," Stephanie replied. "I'm going to need all the help I can get."

"You couldn't find anyone better for the job," Henri remarked pleasantly. "My wife knows more about the functions of the monarchy than I do."

"Possibly because she takes more interest." Morgan's mouth tightened.

Henri smiled at Stephanie. "As you can see, my brother disapproves of me. But younger sons only become important when the older one pops off, and Phillipe is disgust-ingly healthy." The observation was made humorously, with no hidden rancor.

"It would be nice if you'd prepare yourself for the possibility," Morgan commented with thinly concealed impatience.

Henri grinned. "I don't believe in being overtrained. Besides, what's the point? In a year or so I'll drop down to second in line."

Stephanie didn't want her first night to be disrupted by an ongoing family argument, so she said hastily, "I understand you have a little girl."

"Yes, she was waiting to meet you, but I finally sent her upstairs to have dinner," Lydia said.

"I'm afraid time rather got away from us." Morgan's eyes twinkled as they met Stephanie's. "We had a rather important matter to clear up, didn't we, my love?"

"That's understandable." Henri kept a straight face, but he clearly knew what had taken place. "We're honored that you made the effort to see us at all this evening."

"You'll understand if we don't stay long." Morgan grinned.

"Tell Nana to send Paulette down," Lydia instructed her husband quickly.

Their daughter was a beautiful six-year-old with long blond hair. She was also extremely sulky. "I was watching television," she complained.

"That can wait." Lydia's tone must have been uncharacteristically abrupt, because the small girl gave her a startled look. "This is the lady Uncle Phillipe is going to marry. What do you say?"

"I'm very happy to make your acquaintance," Paulette said obediently, dropping a curtsy at her mother's sharp glance.

"It's delightful to meet you, too," Stephanie responded. "I'm very fond of young girls. I was a teacher in my own country."

"You were a tradesperson?" Paulette stared at her incredulously.

Stephanie tried not to laugh. "Well, we call it a profession, but I suppose it's the same thing."

"It isn't the same at all!" Lydia was appalled. "You must excuse her. She's never known anyone who...I mean..."

"It's quite all right." Stephanie took pity on the flustered woman. "I'm just as amazed when I find out someone *doesn't* work. It's merely a difference in cultures."

"Will you teach school in Verlaine?" Paulette asked curiously.

Stephanie smiled at her. "No, but I'm sure I'll find plenty to do."

"Planning the wedding will keep you terribly busy," Lydia agreed.

"I hope your offer was sincere, because I don't know where to begin."

Lydia's eyes brightened. "I did jot down a few ideas in case you were interested."

"I'd be everlastingly grateful," Stephanie assured her.

"This is boring." Paulette was regarding them disapprovingly. "Can I go back upstairs now?"

"That isn't polite, darling," Lydia reproved her mildly. "You may go after you say good-night to Uncle Phillipe and Miss Blair."

"Don't you have a title?" the child asked Stephanie. "*I'm* a princess."

Morgan's face was stormy. "You're addressing your future queen," he said icily.

"She didn't mean to be disrespectful," Lydia said nervously after the chastened child had left.

"I'm sure she didn't," Stephanie soothed. "We'll all take some getting used to."

She smoothed over the awkward moment by steering the conversation back to the wedding. They discussed generalities for a short time while the brothers talked about sports. That was one subject they agreed on, at least.

Finally Morgan said, "This has been a long day for Stephanie. I'm going to order a light supper in our quarters and let her get some rest."

When they were alone in her apartment he said, "Well, what do you think of them? Be honest," he added.

"I liked Henri. He's charming."

Morgan flung himself into a chair, scowling. "I hate to say it about my own brother, but he's a weakling."

"Not really. I got quite the opposite impression."

"How can you say that? Did he utter one word to that *enfant terrible* he sired?"

"Paulette is the one I'm sorry for," Stephanie said soberly.

"The child is a monster!"

"No, she's simply never been taught manners. A few months at Miss Waycroft's would do wonders for her." She smiled.

"That's a job for her parents. Which confirms what I said about Henri. If he can't manage his own family, perhaps it's fortunate that he doesn't take an active part in government. You heard him admit that Lydia knows more about it than he does."

"That's because she enjoys power. Henri doesn't. There have to be leaders and followers in life, and Henri is a follower. He's quite comfortable with the fact. It's you and

Lydia who are unhappy. Henri is doing exactly what he wants to do."

Morgan looked startled. "You really think so? He doesn't resent me?"

"Not in the slightest. I don't believe he wants authority. He was probably attracted to Lydia because she's strong."

Morgan's face set in familiar lines. "That's one word for her."

"She's not so bad. It was very nice of her to offer to help me get adjusted, especially since I'm usurping her position. I think you'll see a big change in her after we're married and she realizes there's no hope of her husband ascending the throne."

Morgan's expression changed as he pulled her onto his lap. "We have to have children before that's a certainty."

"Don't you think we ought to wait till we're married?" she teased.

"We can practice," he murmured, blowing gently in her ear.

"That's one of *your* better ideas." Stephanie lowered her head to reach for his lips.

Chapter Seven

Stephanie's first week in Verlaine was like a vacation at a plush resort. She was waited on hand and foot, and Morgan devoted the entire week to her. The days were spent getting acquainted with the city he loved—and wanted her to love, too—and the nights were filled with romance.

Making a tour of the castle was an experience in itself. Morgan might feel it was a home, not a museum, but the ground floor greatly resembled one. Huge reception rooms and great halls were filled with artwork and priceless tapestries. The lovely antique furnishings were of equal quality.

Corridors with both classic and contemporary sculpture led from the main building to the wings that stretched out on either side. The splendor of the interior was matched by the stunning view of the grounds visible through tall windows framed by silken draperies.

"I'll never find my way around by myself," Stephanie exclaimed. "If I don't show up for a couple of days, send out a St. Bernard with a keg of brandy around his neck."

"We do have a St. Bernard, but he's a disgrace to his breed. The only thing he can find is his dinner dish." Morgan chuckled.

"Where *are* the dogs? I want to see them."

He hadn't exaggerated their number. The kennels were swarming with dogs of every breed. They all started to bark at once when they saw Morgan, and for a short time bedlam reigned.

Stephanie patted the wagging rumps of Great Danes, Labradors and German shepherds; most of the dogs were large. Her special favorite was a black standard poodle named Pepe. Unlike the others, he had immense dignity. His expression was disdainful as he watched the frenzy of hero worship indulged in by his kennel mates.

"Pepe reminds me of you," Stephanie told Morgan as she stroked the poodle's curly topknot. "Except that his eyelashes are longer."

"I don't see the resemblance." He looked critically at the beautiful animal.

"Not physically. I meant you both have that aloof, autocratic manner."

"Come back to the house and I'll show you how wrong you are," he murmured, putting his arm around her waist and drawing her against his lean body.

The idyllic week was a grace period before the world intruded on them with a vengeance. After the short breathing space, a formal announcement of their engagement was made and the wedding date set. That sparked a round of festivities and official occasions to introduce Stephanie to the court and her future subjects. The first event was a grand reception at the castle, arranged by Lydia.

"I hope you don't mind," she said anxiously. "So many people have been asking when they'll get to meet you that it was becoming rather awkward fending them off."

"I understand," Stephanie said. "It's been heavenly having Morgan all to myself this week, but I knew he came with a price tag." She smiled at him.

"I hope you won't think it's too high," he answered.

"I imagine you know the answer to that." Her melting gaze reminded him of their previous night together.

"I've been wanting to ask. Why do you call him Morgan?" Lydia asked curiously.

"It's sort of a nickname. That was the name of the first man I ever fell in love with," Stephanie answered with a straight face.

Lydia looked faintly shocked, but when Morgan merely laughed, she changed the subject hurriedly. "Yes, well...about the reception. It will be formal, of course."

"Oh, dear, here we go again," Stephanie lamented. "I have nothing to wear."

"That's what you said last time, and then you turned up looking ravishing. I think that's something women say automatically," Morgan teased.

"Except that in my case it's true. Will you go shopping with me, Lydia?"

The other woman gazed at her disapprovingly. "Royalty does not buy off the rack."

"Royalty better this time, or the future queen will show up in a bathrobe," Stephanie asserted. "That's the only thing I have that reaches the floor."

Lydia stared at her thoughtfully. "It's too late to get anything from a couturier in time, but I'll have them submit sketches so you can select a wardrobe for future use.

In the meantime, I have a dressmaker who can whip up a few things to tide you over.''

That afternoon a competent older woman arrived at the castle with samples of materials. Lydia joined them in Stephanie's sitting room to help her design a suitable gown for the reception. Soon fabric samples were draped over the sofa and chairs, and sketches covered most of the tables. Stephanie finally began to appreciate the luxury of having her own apartment to clutter up as she wished.

Lydia was very knowledgeable about fashion, but more importantly, she knew what was required for the occasion. When Stephanie would have selected something simple, Lydia explained why it wouldn't be suitable.

"This is your debut. If you don't wear something utterly smashing, people will think you're dressing down for them. It would be a subtle insult, to them and to Morgan."

"I never would have thought of such a thing," Stephanie said slowly.

"You couldn't be expected to. You've never been involved in court politics."

"Or any other kind. I'm afraid I'm going to make the most frightful gaffes."

"Don't worry about it. The people love Phillipe, and he's obviously wild about you. They'll make allowances, especially since you're a foreigner."

"I don't want them to feel sorry for him for marrying a klutz." Stephanie's face was troubled.

"I don't think anyone will feel sorry for him," Lydia observed dryly. "Besides, you won't be completely on your own. I'll brief you on who is important, and what subjects to avoid. I'll be right next to you in the receiving line."

"That's awfully good of you." Stephanie hesitated for a moment. "You really enjoy this sort of thing, don't you?"

"It grows on you."

Stephanie decided to be direct. "If Morgan hadn't chosen to marry, you would still be the ranking lady of the court. I'm surprised you don't resent me. In fact, I expected you to."

Lydia shrugged. "I can't say I'm thrilled about the situation, but it would have been unreasonable to expect Phillipe to remain single all his life. He's been greatly sought after, as you can imagine. It was only a matter of time."

"You're going out of your way to be helpful, though."

"I'm a realist," Lydia answered bluntly. "You're his choice, and there's nothing I can do about it. Making an enemy of you would be stupid."

Stephanie felt slightly chilled. "At least you're honest."

Lydia smiled suddenly. "It's nothing personal. There's no reason why we can't be friends."

When she thought about it later, Stephanie decided she liked Lydia's directness better than her obsequiousness. Morgan would probably like her better, too, if she stopped flattering him to his face and resenting him behind his back. Palace intrigue went out with the Medicis.

Butterflies were holding a convention in Stephanie's stomach on the night of the reception. She wanted so much for Morgan's people to like her.

He'd come upstairs late and was showering while she put the finishing touches to her makeup and hair. She was completely dressed when he came into their bedroom wearing only a towel around his middle.

"I have to tell you about—" He stopped abruptly when he caught sight of her.

The pale blue satin dress molded closely to her bosom and waist before flaring out in a full skirt with just the suggestion of a train. Tiny seed pearls and crystal bugle beads were embroidered in a floral design that edged the low sweetheart neckline and was repeated on the cuffs of the long, pointed sleeves. The effect was regal, combined with her erect carriage, although that was due to tension.

"Do I look all right?" she asked anxiously.

"You look like a queen," he said huskily, touching her cheek with gentle fingers.

"I feel terribly overdressed, but Lydia said this is what people would expect."

"She's right."

"I wouldn't have known if she hadn't advised me. Lydia's been very helpful, Morgan."

"That's a pleasant surprise," he said shortly.

"I wish you wouldn't be so hard on her. It must be very difficult having to step down. She even admitted as much to me, but she's really trying. This reception tonight took a lot of planning. She didn't have to do it."

"Maybe you're right," Morgan admitted. "I'd be delighted to see a change in her. We might turn out to be one happy family after all—except for Paulette. That kid is a horror!"

Stephanie laughed. "Don't say that. You don't know how yours will turn out."

"Not like that. If necessary I'll send them to military school for some strict discipline."

"You've decided we're going to have sons?"

"I don't care what they are," he said tenderly. "I'll cherish them because they're ours, born of our love."

"That's beautiful, darling. I'm looking forward to having your children," she said softly.

"I'd love to oblige you." He put his arms around her waist.

She held him off reluctantly. "We have an engagement party to go to."

"I can think of better ways to celebrate," he grumbled. "But you're right. I'll be ready in five minutes."

He was darkly handsome when he rejoined her in a white dinner jacket and dark trousers. Strains of music were drifting down from the upper floor, but he stopped her as she started for the door.

Taking her left hand, he slipped a ring on her third finger. "Now it's official." He smiled.

She looked down at the huge emerald surrounded by flashing diamonds. "Oh, Morgan, it's gorgeous!"

"I hoped you'd like it. This was my mother's engagement ring, so it has special meaning for me."

She threw her arms around his neck. "I'll treasure it always. And some day it will go to *our* son's wife."

"That's a very lovely thought." He brought her fingers to his lips and kissed them.

The reception was held in the grand ballroom on the third floor of the castle. The huge room was decorated with flowers and scores of tall candles, which cast a flattering glow. A string quartet played during cocktails, and a full orchestra succeeded them later for dancing. Lydia had done a masterful job in a very short time.

Stephanie had trouble believing this was actually her home. She felt as though she'd wandered into a private party where she didn't know anybody, but the reception wasn't as intimidating as she anticipated. While it was true that everyone was curious about her, they seemed inclined to give her the benefit of the doubt.

Lydia's help was invaluable. As the guests came through the receiving line she whispered appropriate comments.

"That's the minister of education. Tell him you're going to work for more funding for schools. He'll be thrilled."

"Is money available?" Stephanie asked.

"Just do it," Lydia urged impatiently.

Stephanie mentioned her background in teaching instead, not wanting to make any commitments before she knew what she was talking about. But her credentials were well received. There wasn't time for more than a few words, anyway, before the next guest was presented.

In brief, pithy asides, Lydia instructed her on the different ranks of royalty and the relative importance of the various ministers of government. After the dignitaries came the socially prominent members of the kingdom. It was all quite confusing, but whenever Stephanie felt herself floundering, Morgan squeezed her hand.

Her most critical scrutiny came from the young, beautiful women who passed through the receiving line. Stephanie knew that many of them must have hoped they'd be standing where she was, but it didn't bother her. She gazed at them with a gracious smile that covered her own speculation.

Guesswork wasn't necessary when a stunning brunette paused in front of Morgan. They obviously knew each other well. He clasped both her hands and gave her a special smile, which she returned in kind. Their voices were muted as they exchanged greetings, creating a small pool of intimacy, although their words were innocent enough.

"It's good to see you again, Alicia," he said. "I'm glad you could come."

"How could I pass up an opportunity to wish you happiness? You're my king," she said softly.

"I prefer to think of myself as your friend," he answered gently.

Stephanie turned to Lydia with a questioning look. Her future sister-in-law was watching the other two with sudden interest. "Later," she murmured.

Morgan reclaimed Stephanie's attention by presenting the woman. "I'd like you to meet an old friend, Lady Alicia LeBec. My fiancée, Stephanie Blair."

The two women inspected each other covertly as they exchanged pleasantries. Lady Alicia had a model's figure with a face to match. Slightly tilted dark eyes and high cheekbones gave an exotic touch to her beauty. Stephanie wasn't surprised that Morgan had been attracted to her. The question was, how deeply had they been involved?

There was no time to puzzle over it at the moment because the receiving line still stretched out lengthily. When the final guest had been welcomed and they were free to move around, Henri grinned at Stephanie.

"If that didn't discourage you, it must be true love."

"I rather enjoyed myself," she answered. "Especially meeting Morgan's old friends."

"Some are older than others," Henri said with a mischievous glance at his brother.

"I was rather surprised at a few who accepted," Lydia remarked.

"We'd better join our guests," Morgan said impassively.

From then on Stephanie was busy trying to remember names and match them to faces. She danced with young men and old, responded to numerous toasts and listened to the reminiscences of old ladies who remembered when Morgan was born.

He was equally busy, moving from one group to another, exchanging a few words, never staying long in one place. The exception was when he danced with Lady Alicia.

Stephanie felt an uncharacteristic stirring of jealousy as she watched the handsome couple. He was holding her in a conventional embrace, certainly not too tightly. Yet their bodies moved in perfect harmony, as though he'd held her in his arms often. Stephanie's smile at the people surrounding her became rather fixed.

She and Morgan didn't have time for more than a few moments together until the party was over and they were in their bedroom. They slept in his bed because he preferred it, and she didn't care one way or the other as long as they were together.

Stephanie went into her dressing room to hang up her ball gown. When she returned in a filmy nightgown, Morgan was shrugging off his shirt. He held out his arms to her.

"Come here. I've been wanting to hold you all evening."

She put her arms around his waist and rubbed her cheek against the crisp tangle of hair on his chest. "I couldn't tell. Sometimes you seemed like a stranger tonight."

"That's because I was practicing self-control. This is what I wanted to do." He drew her closer.

"Was I all right?"

"You were magnificent. Everyone loved you, just as I predicted."

"Even your old girlfriends?"

"You're the only woman in my life." He tilted her chin up and kissed her lingeringly.

She was tempted to drop the subject, but a perverse imp goaded her on. "Lady Alicia is very beautiful," she remarked with apparent innocence.

"She's not in your class." He cupped a hand around her breast and nibbled on her ear.

Stephanie had a suspicion that Morgan was motivated as much by a desire to distract her as by passion. "How well did you know her?"

"Does it matter?" he murmured.

"No, but I'd like to know. I have a feeling it's something everyone else knows."

He stifled a sigh. "Alicia and I are merely good friends. We've known each other all our lives. Her father is my minister of natural resources."

"Is she married to that man she was with? I didn't get his name."

"No, he was her escort for the evening. She was married briefly after—" He stopped abruptly. "She's divorced."

His inadvertent slip was revealing. Alicia had gotten married after she and Morgan broke up. On the rebound? To show him she didn't care? But the marriage didn't last, and she'd never remarried. Was she still hoping?

"There isn't anything between us," Morgan said gently.

"If you say so," Stephanie answered too politely, trying to banish the image of them dancing together with remembered enjoyment.

"You're making a big deal out of nothing," he said impatiently.

"I'm not stupid, Morgan. I saw how you looked at each other tonight."

He hesitated. "All right, we were more than friends. Alicia is a lovely, generous lady. I tried to fall in love with her, but I couldn't. Can't you simply leave it at that?"

"If you're sure it's over," Stephanie said in a small voice.

He stared at her in frustration. "Surely you can't believe I'm carrying a torch for someone else? You're the one I want to spend my life with, the only woman I ever proposed to."

His impassioned statement put everything into perspective. Naturally Morgan had known other women, but she was the one he'd chosen. It was a miracle, and one shouldn't question miracles.

"I'm sorry," she whispered. "It's just that she's so much more glamorous and assured. I couldn't bear to lose you now."

He lifted her in his arms and carried her over to the bed. "Dear heart, it's the other way around. I'm terrified that you'll change your mind and leave *me*."

"I couldn't ever, my love." She stroked his cheek tenderly.

He stared down at her intently and repeated something he'd said the first time they made love. "You're mine, and I'll never let you go."

Any lingering doubts dissolved in a warm rush of love. Stephanie smiled beguilingly. "I believe that's settled, and it's getting late. Don't you think we should go to bed?"

"In addition to your other talents, you're a mind reader." His eyes started to glow as he slipped a lacy strap down her shoulder.

Morgan had laid down strict ground rules long ago. Although Henri and Lydia lived in the castle, they kept to their wing and afforded Morgan privacy. The times the two couples got together were strictly by invitation on Morgan's part. And now Stephanie's.

The next morning she invited them to have brunch in the small garden room she and Morgan used for informal dining. The charming octagonal-shaped room looked out on banks of peonies and roses, whose sweet scent drifted in the open windows. Stephanie felt guilty but gratified that Paulette was having classes with her tutor and couldn't join them.

Stephanie was getting used to having her every whim gratified, although she didn't take undue advantage. She'd ordered brunch to be served, thinking it was a simple request. An elaborate meal was presented, however. Silver chafing dishes held shirred eggs, sautéed mushrooms and bacon. Beautifully garnished platters were layered with a variety of cold meats and cheeses, and other platters held smoked and pickled fish. The baskets of buttered toast and assorted muffins were accompanied by sweet butter and strawberry jam. Melon and several kinds of berries were offered for dessert, in addition to three different kinds of coffee cake.

The previous night's reception was the inevitable topic of conversation. They discussed the guests, giving Stephanie a little background on the more interesting ones. The men lost interest, however, when the women started to talk about the more notable gowns at the party. Morgan excused himself to go to his office, and Henri left to play tennis.

When they were alone, Lydia poured herself another cup of coffee. "I didn't get a chance to answer your questions about Alicia LeBec last night, and I didn't want to mention her name in front of Phillipe."

"Why not?"

Lydia became intent on stirring her coffee. "No reason. I shouldn't have said that."

"I know they had a relationship," Stephanie said calmly.

"You didn't hear it from me." Lydia looked up warily.

"I didn't have to. Anyone could see they'd meant something to each other at one time. I don't think you can hide a thing like that, even after it's over."

"She got married briefly after they broke up," Lydia said casually. "It didn't last long, though."

"I know. Morgan told me."

"I've always wondered what happened between Phillipe and her. Not that it matters now. Alicia must know she's lost out. At least I hope so, for her sake as well as yours."

Stephanie looked sharply at the other woman. Was Lydia trying to make trouble? But that was absurd. Why would she be so helpful if she hadn't accepted the fact of Morgan's coming marriage? Of course, that was before she'd seen him with Alicia again.

Stephanie was suddenly impatient with herself. Lydia was simply a very tactless woman. She knew a lot about protocol, and very little about the sensibilities of the people involved.

"I'm sure Morgan and Alicia thought they were in love at the time, but obviously they weren't. When it's the real thing you know it," she said confidently.

Lydia's expression was enigmatic as she gazed at Stephanie's serene face. "You're a very rare person. Most women would be less than delighted to have an old flame turn up at their engagement party."

Stephanie's smile held the memory of shared passion. "Morgan chose *me*. That might be hard for many people to understand, but it's a fact they'll have to get used to. Some of them might try to cause misunderstandings between us, but they won't succeed."

"You have a lot of self-confidence."

"Actually I have too little. Morgan is the one who gave me assurance."

After a moment's silent evaluation, Lydia said, "It's nice to have a fiancé who's so supportive. Why don't we start making plans for the wedding?"

After the engagement party Stephanie was caught up in a constant round of social and state events. She was the guest of honor at numerous teas, charity events and receptions.

Lydia guided her through the unfamiliar maze and supervised her wardrobe. Between Lydia's dressmaker and the couturiers of Europe, Stephanie was soon supplied with outfits for every occasion. Her wedding gown was commissioned from a famous designer, and the mechanics of a royal wedding were set in motion.

The two women would probably never have been friends if circumstances hadn't thrown them together. They were complete opposites in every way. Yet as the weeks passed, a tentative friendship developed between them. Lydia unbent greatly, even to the extent of showing flashes of dry humor every now and then.

Stephanie was delighted by the warming of their relationship. She began to feel really accepted in her adopted land. Even Morgan noticed the difference in Lydia. He was so gratified by it that his caustic manner toward her changed markedly. The two couples achieved the easy rapport enjoyed by normal families.

As the wedding day approached, things became really hectic. A million details needed attending to, and Stephanie developed typical bride's jitters. She was sure nothing would go smoothly, but Lydia was the calm eye in the middle of the storm. She took care of every crisis as it arose, and even seemed to be enjoying them.

One of the more pleasurable tasks was opening the wedding gifts that poured in. Stephanie was dazzled by the array of antique silver, fragile crystal, heirloom linens and much, much more. They even received a pair of jeweled chalices from the sultan of some far-off land. Everything had to be catalogued so formal thank-you notes could be sent.

"I guess I know what I'll be doing for the rest of the year," Stephanie commented.

"I'll get you a secretary," Morgan promised. "You should also have a personal maid."

"I don't even know what a personal maid does."

"She takes care of your wardrobe and lays out your clothes."

"That doesn't sound like a full-time job. She'd have it easier than *I* do."

"But you have special perks," Morgan said smugly.

"You mean I get to sleep with the king?" Stephanie looked at him disapprovingly. "That's really chauvinistic."

"Then maybe I ought to extend the same privileges to the maid." His eyes danced with mischief.

"Don't even think about it—or anyone else. I don't share," she said firmly.

Morgan's amusement died as he took her in his arms. "Why would I ever want anyone else?"

Stephanie's sister and brother-in-law arrived a few days before the wedding. She'd spoken on the phone with Eloise and Spenser regularly since she left home, but this was the first time they'd seen each other in weeks.

It was a joyous reunion. The sisters had always been close, even though they were different in every way. Eloise had inherited their father's dark hair and eyes, and his pragmatic way of dealing with problems. She was the realist, her younger sister the romantic, although Stephanie had an inner strength that some people missed.

"I can't believe you're really here!" Stephanie threw her arms around her sister.

"And *I* can't believe this place." Eloise looked around Stephanie's elegant sitting room. "I'm going home and throw rocks at our house."

"You sure make it tough on a guy." Spenser grinned. "I had Ellie convinced that she was well off."

"She is," Stephanie said sincerely. "I never thought I'd be lucky enough to be as happy as you two."

"You deserve it," he answered fondly. A genuine affection existed between them.

Morgan had tactfully left them alone after greeting his guests warmly. He'd sent a limousine to meet them at the airport, and ordered their suite at the castle supplied with every comfort. But after seeing that they were taken care of, he disappeared into his office. That evening the whole group, including Henri and Lydia, had dinner together in the stately dining room.

"We're so thrilled to meet our new queen's family," Lydia said to Eloise. "You must be very proud of her."

"We always have been," Eloise answered coolly.

Stephanie winced. Why couldn't Lydia be herself? Flattery wasn't her forte. She always came across as such a phony when she tried it, and she was really quite direct.

"You and Lydia have a lot in common," she told her sister hurriedly. "You're both so organized. Lydia is handling the whole wedding."

"That sounds like quite a job," Eloise commented politely.

"It is, but I enjoy doing it. I was happy to take over," Lydia answered.

Eloise eyed her speculatively. "It can't leave you much time for yourself, in addition to your other duties. Doesn't royalty have to make a lot of ceremonial appearances?"

"Those are Stephanie's responsibilities now," Lydia replied evenly.

Stephanie laughed. "She gives me the important things to do—like cutting ribbons at supermarket openings."

"You're lucky. I get to award the blue ribbons at the county fair." Henri grinned.

Lydia didn't share their amusement. "If anyone would prefer my duties I'll be glad to turn them over."

"We were only teasing, *chérie*," Henri soothed. "What would we do without you?"

Morgan changed the subject. "I'm so happy you could be here to give Stephanie moral support," he said to his guests. "I'm sure she feels overwhelmed at times."

"We wouldn't have missed the wedding for anything, but don't underestimate my little sister," Eloise responded. "After keeping Miss Waycroft's young terrors in line, she can handle any challenge."

"You better believe it." Spenser laughed. "The Blair girls are awesome."

"Don't give away the family secrets before the wedding," Stephanie admonished. "I have him hooked, but not landed yet."

Morgan gave her a sultry look across the table. "You're the one who would have trouble getting away."

Spenser was gratified by their obvious love. "I'm sure the wedding will come off on schedule," he said indulgently.

"Of course it will," Eloise declared. "I'm not going to be cheated out of my role as matron of honor."

After a glance at his wife's set face, Henri said hurriedly, "You're lucky your function is strictly decorative. I'm responsible for handing Phillipe the ring, which I'll probably drop." His laugh didn't quite ring true.

Eloise was puzzled by the tension in both of them. "I suppose you'll be one of the bridesmaids." Her remark to Lydia was tentative.

"No, I'm not in the wedding party," Lydia answered tonelessly.

"You'd better try on your gown as soon as possible," Stephanie told her sister hastily. "In case it needs any alterations."

When dinner was over a little later she and Eloise went up to her sitting room. Lydia declined an invitation to join them, and the men stayed downstairs.

"I have a feeling I said something wrong down there," Eloise remarked. "Surely you asked Lydia to be one of your bridesmaids?"

"Of course I asked her, but she's a princess." Stephanie sighed. "They have to have a special place in the pecking order, and there wasn't one."

"Except matron of honor," Eloise said slowly.

"Exactly."

Eloise hesitated. "I'm not being noble, but if it's causing trouble, I'll step aside."

"Absolutely not!" Stephanie was very firm on the point. "This is my wedding, and you're going to be my attendant. Lydia could have been a bridesmaid without losing face, or whatever she thought it would do to her image. We could have ordered a special gown to point up her rank."

"That's an idea. Did you suggest it?"

"Yes, but she refused. So it's her choice, not mine."

"You might have made an enemy," Eloise cautioned. "Watch out for that woman, Stephanie."

"She's really not so bad."

"Compared to what?" Eloise asked with a raised eyebrow.

"No, honestly. I understand Lydia. I can handle her."

"By removing the poison sac behind her fangs?" Eloise inquired dryly.

"It's not like you to be so uncharitable," Stephanie reproved her.

"That's because you're my sister, and I care about you. Getting married is enough of an adjustment without having a tricky relative plotting a palace coup."

"You're being ridiculous," Stephanie said impatiently. "Lydia and I get along fine, and when I return from my honeymoon we'll get along even better. I plan to turn over a lot of my duties to her." She grinned suddenly. "Why should I have all the fun snipping ribbons at supermarkets?"

"She really likes that sort of thing?"

"Laps it up."

"Then by all means give her a pair of scissors and keep her happy."

"Now that I've eased your mind, you can try on your dress."

Whatever else Eloise thought about Lydia, she had to admit the other woman had done a masterful job on her gown. It was a deep shade of coral with simple, elegant lines. Stephanie disclaimed any credit for selecting it.

"Lydia has wonderful taste," she said. "You should see the wardrobe she ordered for me. Everything is stunning."

"Maybe I misjudged her," Eloise admitted, turning to look at herself from another angle. "This dress is certainly beautiful. It fits perfectly, too."

"I told Lydia what colors I liked and let her do the rest. The bridesmaids' gowns are a lighter shade than yours. I think the color will be flattering to everyone. The bouquets will have salmon-colored roses and white stephanotis, with satin streamers in both shades."

Eloise unzipped her dress and stepped out of it carefully. "Your gown is the one I want to hear about," she said as she put on her own clothes again.

"It's here. Would you like to see it?"

"I can't wait!"

"I won't try it on because it has endless little buttons down the front that take forever to fasten, but I'll show it to you."

The gown she took from the closet had a voluminous white satin skirt ending in a long train. The close-fitting bodice was made of reembroidered lace, which looked even more fragile in contrast to the heavy, creamy satin. Both the design and workmanship were superb, a tribute to the famous couturier who had created it.

"Oh, Steffie, it's exquisite!" Eloise declared. "You'll look like a fairy princess."

Stephanie grinned. "I'm supposed to look like a queen, but I guess I can settle for princess."

"You don't have to *settle* for anything," Eloise stated firmly. "You have it all."

Stephanie's eyes were dreamy as she hugged the dress to her breast. "All I really care about is Morgan. Isn't he wonderful?"

"He's quite a hunk," Eloise agreed. "But better than that, he loves you just as much."

"Did your sister go to bed?" Morgan's voice preceded him a moment before he appeared in the doorway of the dressing room.

"Morgan! You shouldn't be here," Stephanie exclaimed.

He looked confused since they were both fully dressed. "I'm sorry. When I knocked and no one answered, I wasn't sure you were here."

"You're not supposed to see the bridal gown before the wedding," she said agitatedly. "It's bad luck."

"That's an old wives' tale," Eloise soothed. "Besides, it isn't the gown, it's the bride *wearing* the gown, and you're not."

"That's just a technicality," Stephanie fretted.

"My darling Stephanie, how can anything bring us bad luck?" His voice was deeply resonant.

After viewing the light in his eyes Eloise remarked casually, "Well, I think I'll turn in. It's been a long day."

Morgan reached for Stephanie before the sitting-room door closed.

Chapter Eight

After that first night, Stephanie and her family had little time to visit together. The few days before the wedding were filled with rehearsals, a constant round of parties and a million last-minute details. More gifts arrived, the telephone rang constantly, and minor problems arose and were resolved. Then finally, after all the frantic activity, the wedding day arrived.

In spite of all the preparations, Stephanie had a feeling of unreality as she stood in the middle of her mirrored dressing room while Eloise and Lydia helped her into her gown. A stranger stared back at her from a dozen different angles, a slender woman with wide green eyes and impeccably groomed auburn hair.

"Don't be nervous," Eloise advised. Her own fingers were shaking as she tried to fasten the tiny satin-covered buttons on Stephanie's bodice. "You'll be just fine."

Stephanie smiled at her sister. "I'm not nervous."

She had been up to that moment, terrified that her happiness would be snatched away at the last minute. But all the things she'd worried about had been hobgoblins of her own imagination. Nothing bad was going to happen. She and Morgan would love each other for the rest of their lives.

"There, that does it." Lydia stepped back to stare at her critically. "You're all ready, and on time, too. The car is waiting, and your bouquet is already at the church." She was like a stage manager urging her actors onstage.

Stephanie paused. "I wish you were taking part in the ceremony."

Lydia smiled unexpectedly. "I've done everything but walk down the aisle for you. What more do you want?"

"I'd like to share my happiness with you."

Lydia was momentarily speechless. She finally answered in a softened tone, "That's a nice thing to say, but this is your day. Enjoy it." She gave Stephanie an uncharacteristically mischievous look. "I know *I* would."

As the first strains of the bridal march sounded, Stephanie started down the long, red-carpeted aisle on her brother-in-law's arm. She was only vaguely conscious of the sea of faces turned toward her in the lovely vaulted cathedral. Huge bouquets of white roses and lilies on tall standards lined the aisle, and more flowers banked the distant altar. As she made her slow procession, a ray of sunlight slanted through a stained-glass window and turned her hair the glowing color of claret. A low murmur rippled through the huge crowd, but Stephanie's full attention was on the tall man waiting at the altar for her.

She lifted her veil when she joined him, and their eyes met. He took her hand and held it as the long ceremony began. It was solemn, yet uplifting, a celebration of the present and the future. The pressure of Morgan's fingers increased as the final words that joined them together were spoken. When it was over he kissed her with a love that needed no words.

After that the festivities began in earnest. As Stephanie and Morgan emerged from the church, television cameras began to whir and photographers jostled for position. Hundreds of people were waiting outside for a glimpse of the royal couple.

Stephanie and Morgan waved and smiled as they got into an open carriage for a procession through the city.

He squeezed her hand. "Thank God that's over. Now we can settle down to some peace and quiet—at least after this day is finished. Do you think you can hold up a little longer?"

"I'm enjoying myself. I believe I'm going to like being a queen."

"I guarantee it," he murmured in her ear.

"Behave yourself," she admonished. "You're supposed to act in a kingly manner in front of your people."

"They not only understand, they approve." He grinned. "Where do you think little kings and queens come from?"

"How can you bring that up at a time like this?" she chided, continuing to wave at the cheering throngs lining the streets.

He chuckled. "You inspire me."

Eventually they returned to the castle for the wedding reception, which went on for hours. The many large rooms were filled to capacity with well-wishers eager to toast the newlyweds.

Stephanie appreciated the sentiment, but her feet were beginning to hurt and her face felt stretched from wearing a perpetual smile. As she was wondering if she could at least change her shoes, Morgan came over to her.

"I think we can slip away if we do it unobtrusively," he said in a low voice.

"I thought you'd never ask!"

"That sounds promising."

"My shoes are pinching," she explained.

"You sure know how to hurt a guy." He laughed.

"Where shall I meet you after I change?" she asked.

"I'll be out by the garage. Use the back stairs."

Stephanie located her sister and signaled to her discreetly. Eloise nodded and joined her upstairs a few moments later.

"I wish we could have spent more time together," Stephanie said as she hung up her wedding gown and reached for a sapphire-blue silk blouse. It matched the lining of her white traveling suit. "It seems as though you just got here."

"To me, too, but we'll be in touch."

"I hope you and Spence will come back soon."

"Or maybe you'll visit us. Although I suppose my friends would freak out now that you're a queen."

"That part's unimportant. Just tell them I married the most wonderful man in the world."

"He's a good person. Be happy, little sister."

"Can you doubt it?"

Eloise hesitated. "You don't have an easy life ahead of you."

"I thought you told me I had it all."

Eloise's face cleared as she looked at the radiant younger woman. "You do. Enjoy every minute."

"I intend to," Stephanie answered confidently.

Morgan was waiting impatiently for her next to a low, sleek sports car. "I was beginning to think I'd have to come in and pull you out bodily."

"I was saying goodbye to Eloise."

"I liked your sister and brother-in-law," he said warmly. "They're great people."

"She said the same thing about you." Stephanie sighed happily. "We have nice families."

"I must admit you've done wonders with Lydia," Morgan said as he drove down the long driveway. "Now if you could do something about Paulette I'll really believe you're a magician. One suggestion would be to turn her into a worm. That's the only thing I can think of that doesn't have a mouth, or at least vocal cords."

"Give me time to work on her," she answered complacently.

Although it was after midnight, the whole city was still celebrating. An occasional Roman candle went off in a backyard, a pale imitation of the earlier public display, but still festive. Lights shone from most of the houses, and music drifted out of open windows.

When they reached the outskirts of town Stephanie said, "Isn't it time you told me where we're going on our honeymoon?"

He turned his head to smile at her. "Where would you like to go?"

"Anywhere that we can be alone together," she answered simply.

"My sentiments exactly." He reached for her hand. "I think I chose the perfect spot, but if you don't like it we can go someplace else tomorrow."

Stephanie was intensely curious. Morgan had been so secretive that he'd even had her luggage packed for her when she asked what kind of clothes she'd need. She was bewildered when he stopped the car and got out to open a locked gate in a tall chain-link fence. They appeared to be in deep wilderness. He wouldn't answer any of her questions, however.

The narrow lane they traveled along ended in a clearing on top of a hill. A low, rustic house was set among tall trees. Welcoming lights shone from all the windows, providing an oasis in the darkness.

"Where are we?" she asked as they walked up the path to the front door.

"This is my secret hideaway." He lifted her in his arms and carried her over the threshold. "And now it's yours, my beautiful bride. Everything I have is yours."

Their kiss was sweet with the knowledge that they had unlimited time together. They savored it, lingered over it, drew out the pleasure.

Finally Morgan lifted his head and smiled at her. "Let me show you around."

The large living room had a beamed ceiling and a huge stone fireplace. There was no dining room, but the spacious kitchen held a round table and chairs. The master bedroom had a distinctly male feeling, like the rest of the house. This was no love nest where Morgan brought his current favorite. It was the refuge of a very private man. She understood that he'd paid her a very special compliment by choosing it for their honeymoon.

He was watching her anxiously as she gazed around at the king-size bed and the absence of frills. "It isn't very luxurious. We can go to a resort if you'd rather. Or maybe Paris or Rome, where there's more excitement."

She put her arms around his neck. "Why would I want to go anywhere else when I have everything I want right here?"

He hugged her tightly. "Do you know how much I love you?"

"As much as I love you?"

"More. When I saw you coming down the aisle you looked like an angel. That's why I held onto your hand. I didn't want you to go back to heaven without me."

She touched his cheek gently. "I'd be so lonely without you."

"Why are we even talking about the possibility? This is only the beginning of our happiness." He framed her face in his palms and gazed at her tenderly. "I'll never stop loving you. Always remember that."

Their lovemaking had a special sweetness that night. It held the same passion—that was a constant between them, an instant flame that could ignite with a glance. But the knowledge that they now belonged to each other without a shadow of a doubt brought an inner kind of peace.

They stroked each other almost languidly at first, postponing the rapture. Then gradually their caresses became more urgent. The kisses Morgan strung out along her body were first pleasurable, then tantalizing and finally, almost unbearably arousing.

She touched him in the same way, stoking his ardor until he was rigid with desire and unable to restrain himself. His possession was eagerly welcomed. Stephanie's wordless little cries of delight were swallowed up in his mouth as their bodies twined and arched against each other. The final explosion was like all the fireworks that had celebrated their union.

Stephanie could smell the rich aroma of coffee before she was fully awake. She opened her eyes when Morgan set a tray down on the bed. It held orange juice and two plates of steaming scrambled eggs and bacon, accompanied by a silver pot of coffee.

"Good morning, Your Majesty." He smiled down at her. "One of your loyal subjects would like a kiss."

She sat up and pushed the tumbled hair out of her eyes. "My, the natives are certainly cheeky. Is that one of the queen's duties?"

He leaned down to kiss her, cupping his hand around her breast. "I'm hoping it will be a pleasure."

"It is," she replied softly.

He drew back a fraction. "If we make love now, your eggs will get cold. But on the other hand, the refrigerator is well stocked."

She glanced at the tray. "I suppose the cook wouldn't be too thrilled."

"Do I look unhappy?"

"*You* made breakfast?"

"Does that surprise you?"

"I don't know why it should," she said fondly. "You can do everything else."

"Some things with more enthusiasm than others," he murmured, reaching for her.

It was an idyllic week, even better than the one in Palm Beach because they were completely alone. There were no outside demands on their time, no schedules to follow. They had picnics in the woods and played backgammon or chess until the early hours of the morning. Nothing was structured. If they woke up hungry in the middle of the night they went into the kitchen together and made simple things like tuna-fish sandwiches, or slightly more elaborate ones like Welsh rarebit flavored with wine.

A lovely trout stream running through the property provided them with some of their best dinners. Morgan showed Stephanie how to tie a lure on a line and cast with a lightweight rod and reel. The thigh-high rubber wading boots he found for her were too big, but she gamely clumped through the water in them to the middle of the stream where he said the biggest trout were.

One day she stepped in a hole and her waders filled with water. There was no danger, but she was anchored firmly in the middle of the stream. Morgan had to lift her out of the boots to free her.

"I don't know why you think it's so funny," she said indignantly when he deposited her on the bank. "I could have drowned!"

"Hardly." He tried to contain his laughter. "The water isn't deep enough."

"A lot of good that is," she muttered, plucking at her wet shirt. "Look at me. I'm soaked."

"The sun will dry you off in no time," he soothed, unbuttoning her shirt.

"It's all your fault for not telling me to watch out for holes." She put her hand on his shoulder to steady herself while she stepped out of her sopping jeans. "A pair of waders my size would be nice, too. The ones you gave me must have been castoffs from the Jolly Green Giant."

Morgan's amused answer was never given. His laughter died as he looked at her slim body clad only in panties and a bra. The cool water had curled her nipples into coral pebbles, clearly visible through the delicate lace, and her wet panties were equally revealing.

He took her in his arms wordlessly, and they made love on the grassy bank in the warm sunshine, which shone down on them like a benediction.

The week was over much too soon. "We can go wherever you like after we get back," Morgan said. "You're certainly entitled to more than a week's honeymoon, but I can't stay incommunicado for any longer than this."

"I understand, darling," she assured him.

"Would you like to go to the Riviera? Or perhaps you'd prefer a cruise."

"No, I'd like to go home and start whipping the castle into shape." She smiled. "Your bedroom needs a woman's touch."

He leered playfully at her. "Feel free to touch anything of mine you want."

"I already have," she answered demurely.

In spite of her avowed intention, Stephanie was slow to assert herself. For a couple of weeks she simply reveled in being a newlywed, devoting most of her time to Morgan. Their presence was required at some state functions, but a good part of the time they had dinner alone in their quarters.

They also spent as much time as possible together during the day. Sometimes they rode horseback with the pack of mismatched dogs loping happily along. Even the big poodle dropped his dignity during their romps in the wood. After some consideration he attached himself to Stephanie, and they were soon inseparable. Pepe became the official palace dog, spoiled and pampered.

"That mutt gets treated better than I do," Morgan complained one afternoon when he came looking for Stephanie.

She was lying on a chaise in her sitting room, reading a book. Pepe was curled up next to her, and she was stroking his head.

"Are you feeling neglected?" she teased.

"No—jealous." He nudged the dog off the chaise and took his place. "I don't intend to share you with anyone."

"Not even your children?"

He gave her a startled look. "Are you trying to tell me something?"

"No, but it's a subject we should discuss."

He grinned. "I don't think a lot of talk is involved."

"Be serious, Morgan. Now that you're married, your people are going to expect an heir to the throne."

"*Our* people," he corrected gently.

"You're right, our people," she apologized.

"I suppose it will take time until you feel like one of us," he said slowly.

"I already do," she assured him earnestly. "It was just a slip of the tongue."

He wasn't convinced. "It's natural to miss your own country, but you can go back for a visit whenever you want."

"Are you trying to get rid of me already?" she demanded.

"I must be doing something wrong if you don't know better than that."

They didn't talk for long moments. Then Stephanie cradled his head on her shoulder and said, "We really have to talk about having a family, Morgan."

"We've only been married a few weeks," he objected mildly.

"I know. I wasn't suggesting anything immediate, but I think we should make plans. I'm not getting any younger."

"You aren't unique in that respect."

She looked at him searchingly. "Don't you want children?"

"Of course I do—especially yours." His gaze was filled with love. "I hope we have at least one little girl who looks exactly like you."

"Then why are you so reluctant to talk about it?"

His former playful manner disappeared when he saw that she was concerned. "I owe it to the monarchy to have children, darling. It's one of my obligations as well as my pleasures. I'm going to love being a father, but right now I'm more interested in being a husband and lover. We have the rest of our lives to serve the country. I don't think it's unreasonable to want to be the most important person in your life for a while."

"That won't ever change."

"I know, but you do understand, don't you?"

Stephanie's heart swelled with love at the evidence that this powerful, sophisticated man had some of the insecurities of ordinary mortals.

"You don't mind waiting a little while, do you?" he persisted.

"No, darling," she said fondly. "I don't mind at all."

Stephanie had everything a woman could wish for, but after a few weeks she started getting restless. She'd always urged her students to make something of their lives. If they didn't need to work for money, they should find something useful to do with their time. She believed in that advice, yet she wasn't taking it herself. The problem was finding something to do that wasn't merely busywork.

She rummaged through the piles of papers on her desk, looking for a list of the requests for her presence. Most of them were largely ceremonial appearances, more social than anything else.

That was Lydia's forte. She was happy as a bee in a rose garden playing the royal princess. Stephanie had no desire to deprive her of the pleasure; that wasn't the sort of thing she was looking for.

An item on the list caught her attention. A children's hospital was asking for a visit by a member of the royal family to give the children a small break in their daily routine. Stephanie could think of a lot of things that would brighten their day more, but she decided to accept.

As soon as she walked into the first ward, Stephanie knew she'd found her niche. The children were shy in the beginning, since the importance of her visit had been stressed. They soon warmed to her, though, when she drew them into conversation.

"Do you have any brothers or sisters?" she asked Michel, an adorable small boy.

He nodded. "I have a new baby sister. That's why my mommy can't come to visit me very often. She has to take care of the baby."

"My mommy can't come because she has to work all day." A little girl in the next bed joined the conversation.

"That's why they looked forward so to your visit," the head nurse confided. "Their days become very monotonous cooped up here without anything to do."

"Isn't there any kind of playroom where they could go for an hour or two?" Stephanie asked.

"Most of them can't get around by themselves, but even if we could take them in wheelchairs, they'd have to be supervised. We simply don't have enough help."

"I appreciate your problem," Stephanie said slowly. "Still, it must be deadly for the poor tykes."

"We try to spend a few minutes with each one every day, but that's no substitute for family visits." The nurse sighed. "I don't know what the answer is."

Michel plucked at Stephanie's sleeve. "You can color in my coloring book if you want, only I used up my green crayon so you can't fill in the trees."

"That's no problem. I'll show you a trick." She sat on the bed next to him and selected a blue crayon and a yellow one from the box he offered her. "When you shade one on top of the other, you get green. See?"

"Will you do my trees like that, too?" the little girl asked eagerly, offering her own book.

"It's time for your therapy, Denise." A nurse prepared to lift her into a wheelchair.

"No! I want to stay and play with the lady." She started to cry.

"I have to leave now," Stephanie said hastily. "But I'll be back. And next time I'll show you how to make orange and purple. Would you like that?" She was rewarded by a nod and a watery smile.

That night Stephanie was filled with a mixture of excitement and indignation as she told Morgan about her day.

"Those poor kids just lie there like turnips, and nobody does anything about it," she said.

He smiled. "I have a feeling you're going to."

"Count on it! What would you think about organizing a volunteer group to read to the children and play games with them?"

"You mean me, personally?" he teased, gazing fondly at her animated face.

She barely heard him. "A lot of elderly people have too much time on their hands. I'll bet they'd jump at the chance. We could enlist teenagers, also. At home we have something called candy stripers. They're very dependable workers."

"It sounds like a fine idea. By all means pursue it."

"I'm going to need some money."

"I thought the word volunteer was mentioned. Or does that only apply to me?" He chuckled.

"It's for a playroom for the children," she explained. "And maybe an outdoor playground, too, so they can get some fresh air."

"I don't think that would put undue stress on the budget," he answered indulgently.

She stared at him thoughtfully. "If I get enough response we can perform the same service in other hospitals, perhaps even homes for the elderly. I'll have to visit some of those."

Morgan grinned. "Well, at least *they* won't need playgrounds."

Stephanie threw herself wholeheartedly into the project. Her phone rang constantly, and she spent most of her days in committee meetings or at the hospital. The activity agreed with her. Her eyes sparkled and she was charged with energy.

On a particularly beautiful summer afternoon Stephanie decided to work on her current project out of doors. She was decorating small baskets to be filled with candy for a party at the hospital the next day. Pepe was lying at her feet on the wide flagstone patio. He lifted his head expectantly, then lowered it with disinterest as Paulette came around the corner.

"What are you doing?" the little girl asked, stopping beside the table.

"Tying ribbons onto these baskets for a party," Stephanie answered.

"Why don't you tell one of the maids to do it?"

"Because it isn't her job, it's mine."

"You don't have to work. You're the queen."

"Everyone should do something, especially queens— and princesses," Stephanie added.

Paulette examined the curious idea silently for a moment. Then she asked, "Why?"

"Because the more fortunate should help those less fortunate. Thinking only of yourself is selfish, besides being boring."

"Is that why people don't like me? Because I'm selfish?"

Stephanie's hands stilled. Paulette might be spoiled, but she certainly wasn't stupid. "What makes you think people don't like you?" she asked casually.

"Nobody wants to play with me." The little girl's voice was matter-of-fact. "They only come to my birthday parties because they have to."

"How do you know that?"

"I heard them talking."

Stephanie picked her way carefully. "Most children enjoy parties. Do you know why they don't want to come to yours?"

Paulette shrugged. "They say I'm too bossy."

"Why do they feel that way?"

"Nobody wants to play the games I do, but I make them, anyway."

"Wouldn't it be more polite to ask your guests what games they want to play?"

Paulette looked at her in mild astonishment. "They have to do what *I* say."

Stephanie suppressed a sigh. This was going to be harder than she anticipated. "That might be true, but it won't win you any friends. If you want people to like you, you have to consider their feelings. I could tell you to go upstairs to your room and you'd have to do it because I outrank you. But it wouldn't make you want to be with me again."

"You mean if I let them choose and have first turn they'd like me?" Paulette asked slowly.

"That's part of it. Mostly, though, it's treating your friends as equals. No one enjoys being dictated to."

Paulette thought it over. "It would be nice to have someone to play with," she said tentatively.

"How would you like to come to the party at the hospital with me tomorrow?" Stephanie asked impulsively. "You can help serve the ice cream and cake."

Paulette's face lit up. "I never did that before."

She was busily helping Stephanie tie bows on the baskets when Lydia showed up. "There you are, my darling. I was looking all over for you."

"I'm helping Aunt Stephanie. She's taking me to a party tomorrow," Paulette announced.

At Lydia's questioning look, Stephanie explained, "It's a birthday party for one of the children at the hospital."

Lydia's reaction was immediate. "Are you out of your mind? God knows what she could catch there!"

"None of them have infectious diseases," Stephanie answered patiently.

"You can't guarantee that. Children are always coming down with something. Besides, I don't want Paulette in that atmosphere. It's too depressing."

"I *want* to go," Paulette protested.

"It's out of the question," Lydia decreed.

As Paulette's lower lip jutted out, Stephanie said placatingly, "It would mean a great deal to the children, and I think Paulette would get a lot out of it, too."

Lydia's body was rigid with anger. "She's my child, and I say no! You might be the queen, but you can't tell me how to raise my daughter. That's *one* thing you can't take over."

Paulette was obviously upset by the clash. Stephanie glanced at her and said pleasantly, "We'll do something else together. Would you do me a favor and take Pepe for a walk? I haven't had time today."

She and Lydia were both silent until the child had left. Then Stephanie said quietly, "She's a very lonely little girl."

"You don't know what you're talking about. She has everything."

"Except friends. You're not doing her a favor by telling her she's better than everyone else because she's a princess."

"She *is*! Paulette has beauty and brains and breeding. Some day my daughter will be married to a monarch. She won't ever have to take second place to anyone!"

That night Stephanie told Morgan about the disagreement. "I understand now why Lydia is so permissive. I always felt it was totally out of character—you'd think she'd be terribly strict. But that child is the embodiment of all her own frustrated ambitions. I never realized how badly she wanted to be queen."

"I thought she was resigned to the fact. She's certainly been pleasanter to live with lately."

"She *is* resigned, for herself. But Paulette is her ace in the hole—Lydia's claim to fame."

Morgan yawned. "Well, it isn't your problem."

"No, but I'm not going to see Paulette cheated out of her childhood," Stephanie answered stubbornly.

He pulled her closer in the big bed. "Maybe I was wrong. Since you're determined to fill your life with children, perhaps it's time we had one of our own."

"Oh, sure! Now that I'm knee-deep in projects, you give in."

He slid one foot up and down her leg. "Why don't we kick the idea around and see what develops?"

Things were a little stiff between the two women for a few days. Lydia remained indignant over the challenge to her authority in the one field she ruled unquestionably. Stephanie went out of her way to be conciliatory, partly to restore peace, but mostly for Paulette's sake.

Making the child's life more normal required a delicate balancing act. She had no right to undermine Lydia's authority, no matter how convinced she was that the woman was wrong. On the other hand, an aunt couldn't be faulted for showing an interest in her niece.

Since Paulette was so disappointed at missing the birthday party at the hospital, Stephanie wanted to give her not only an acceptable substitute, but an exciting one. A week later she had a Christmas party on the castle lawn.

The surrounding pine trees were decorated with brightly colored Christmas ornaments and puffs of cotton to simulate snow. Long wooden tables were covered with holiday cloths printed with holly wreaths and candy canes. Everything was as authentic as possible. The horses attached to Santa's sleigh had fake reindeer horns attached to their heads, but it's doubtful if the children noticed. They were too dazzled by the jolly man in the red suit and his big bag of presents.

"It isn't Christmas, though," Michel pointed out reluctantly. "How come we're having a holiday party in August?"

"I never gave a Christmas party before, so I thought I'd better have a rehearsal," Stephanie explained. "Did I forget anything?" The shining eyes of all the little guests told her she hadn't.

When it was time to give out the gifts, Paulette took them from Santa and handed them to the children. She was more animated than Stephanie had ever seen her. It was probably the first time Paulette had been on the giving instead of the receiving end, and she discovered the pleasure that could bring.

"You're very clever," Lydia said with grudging respect. She and Stephanie were standing on the sidelines watching the festivities.

"What do you mean?" Stephanie asked innocently.

"You brought the mountain to Mohammed."

"I couldn't exclude Paulette from a party here at her own home," Stephanie said carefully. "That would have been cruel. But you didn't have to let her attend."

"Thanks for giving me a choice." Lydia's tone was ironic.

"I don't think you need worry about her catching any germs out here in the open air," Stephanie replied mildly.

That day brought about a change in Paulette. Her behavior was markedly different, although she didn't become an angel overnight. Stephanie knew it wasn't her place to correct someone else's child, but when Paulette said something outrageous, a glance was enough to tell her she'd been rude.

The next step in Stephanie's campaign was to invite various ladies of the court to lunch at the castle with their children. It was a calculated risk. Lydia could take offense at her meddling and turn into a formidable enemy. But as Paulette blossomed into a normal child and became noticeably happier, Lydia remained alert, yet silent.

The only comment she made to Stephanie was vaguely complimentary. "You're so good with children, I'm surprised you haven't started your own family."

Morgan brought up the same subject one night. He stroked Stephanie's flat stomach and looked at her questioningly. "Did you change your mind about wanting a baby?"

"How could I? Isn't that the reason you made an honest woman of me?" she teased.

"One of many." He nibbled delicately on her lower lip. "An heir to the throne was third on the list."

"What were one and two?"

"The main reason I married you was because I love you. The second was because you have the most delectable body I've ever seen."

His lips slid slowly down her neck to the hollow between her breasts, then continued to her navel, where he paused to dip his tongue into the little depression. Stephanie moved her hips in anticipation as Morgan aroused her with loving expertise.

No further conversation took place that night.

Chapter Nine

Stephanie was mildly surprised that she didn't become pregnant immediately, but she supposed it could take a month or two. When time passed without the desired happening, however, she began to get tense.

Lydia noticed and commented on the fact that she seemed nervous. Relations between the two women had smoothed, once Lydia was convinced that Stephanie wasn't subtly plotting to alienate her daughter's affections.

Their priorities were still sharply divergent, but they were thrown together a lot, and they had many of the same interests. An unlikely camaraderie had developed between them.

"You're losing weight," Lydia remarked one day. "If you're dieting, you're overdoing it."

"I'm not dieting," Stephanie answered shortly.

"What's wrong, then? Don't you feel well?"

"I'm fine," Stephanie insisted. "I just have a few problems—with the auxiliary," she added hastily. "I'm late for a meeting right now."

Lydia watched speculatively as she hurried away.

Another week went by before Lydia tentatively broached the subject again. "I don't want to be a nag, but perhaps you should see a doctor. I was watching you at the ambassador's dinner last night. You hardly ate a thing."

"I realize it was a dull evening, but didn't you have anything better to do than that?" Stephanie joked weakly.

"Are you pregnant?" Lydia asked bluntly.

Stephanie's attempt at normality collapsed. "No, that's the whole trouble. I've been trying for months, and nothing has happened."

Something flared in Lydia's eyes and was gone almost immediately. "Is Phillipe upset?"

"I haven't told him." When her sister-in-law raised an eyebrow, Stephanie said, "At first he wanted to wait for a while, and I agreed. He doesn't know I've been trying to get pregnant."

"I see." Lydia's voice was impassive.

"You mustn't tell him!"

"Of course I won't."

"I'm sure there's nothing to worry about." Stephanie's voice was less assured than her words. "It might simply take longer to conceive when you reach your late twenties."

"That could be it. Or maybe you're trying too hard," Lydia soothed. "Why don't you and Phillipe go on a long vacation? That might do it."

"He has that tri-state conference coming up next week, remember? He couldn't possibly get away."

"That's right, I forgot. Well, just try to relax. I'm sure everything will work out."

"Thanks, Lydia. I feel better now that we've talked."

"You should have told me sooner," Lydia scolded. "I knew something was wrong and I was concerned."

"That's good of you," Stephanie said gratefully. "You'll be the first to know after I tell Morgan."

When she left Stephanie, Lydia went to her bedroom and locked the door before making a phone call on her private telephone.

"Dr. Courbet is with a patient now," his nurse informed her. "May I have him return your call?"

"Tell him Princess Lydia is on the line, and I want to talk to him *now*."

A few moments later the doctor's voice greeted her. "It's so nice to hear from you, ma'am. I hope nothing is wrong?"

"No, I'm feeling especially well, and you will be, too. I'm sending you a new patient."

"That's very kind of you."

"Don't you want to know who it is?"

"I can assure you that anyone you recommend will receive my fullest attention."

"Try to restrain your usual instincts, Armand." Lydia smiled nastily. "This one is the queen."

"Queen Stephanie? I'm very flattered to be chosen gynecologist to the queen!" he exclaimed.

"I thought you would be. The title comes with a few conditions, however."

"What are they?" he asked warily.

"It's my duty to see that the queen is not upset," Lydia informed him regally. "So I want you to give me the results of her examination before you give them to her."

"Do you suspect a serious problem?" he asked slowly.

"Not at all. But she's a very high-strung person. In case you do discover something that might distress her, it would be better for me to break the news."

"What you're asking is a breach of confidentiality between doctor and patient," he protested.

"Don't talk to me about confidentiality." Lydia's pretense of geniality dropped as her voice turned cold as steel. "I've kept a secret or two in my day, as you very well know."

Dr. Courbet flushed a dull red as he stared impotently at the phone. After a long moment he said tonelessly, "I'll call you after her visit."

"Thank you, Armand." Lydia switched back to graciousness. "It's so nice to have a friend you can count on."

Her eyes glittered with excitement as she hung up. The runaway emotion was controlled, however, when she joined Stephanie in the flower room where she was arranging roses in a number of vases.

"Aren't they exquisite?" Stephanie inhaled the perfume of a beautiful pink blossom. "I'm sending them to the retirement home. Nothing brightens up a room more than flowers."

"Don't you get tired of doing good deeds?" Lydia asked a trifle acidly.

Stephanie shrugged. "I don't look at it that way. It's silly to let these lovely things die on the bushes when people can get pleasure out of them."

"I hear they're naming the new rose garden in Glenville Park after you."

"It's such a thrill." Stephanie's face was soft. "Not because of the honor. It means the people have accepted me."

"Why shouldn't they? You married their king, and you'll be the mother of the heir to the throne some day."

"I hope so," Stephanie murmured in a low voice.

"Don't be so negative," Lydia chided. "I meant to ask you before. Have you seen a doctor?"

"No. I guess I should, but I've been putting it off. I don't know anyone here."

"I'll give you the name of a good gynecologist," Lydia offered. "I'll even make an appointment for you."

"I don't have time right now," Stephanie objected weakly.

"You can *make* time. It's important to have a regular checkup, especially in your position."

Lydia refused to listen to any excuses. She made an appointment for the next day, and checked to be sure Stephanie kept it.

After the examination Stephanie sat in the doctor's office, gazing at him anxiously. He was in his early forties, handsome and well built, but his appearance didn't register with her.

"Am I all right, Dr. Courbet?" she asked. "Is there any reason why I haven't been able to conceive?"

"You're not to worry about a thing," he soothed. "I want to run a few tests, and then we can have a long talk."

Her knuckles whitened. "That sounds ominous."

"Not at all. It's just doctor talk." He smiled engagingly. "We have to preserve our godlike image."

"I'd really rather know now if you even suspect anything. I'm going to imagine all sorts of things until I hear from you."

"It won't be long," he promised.

"Well, I guess I'll have to be patient." She sighed.

He hesitated. "I'm truly sorry. I wish I could tell you more."

After she left he dialed Lydia's private number. She was waiting by the phone.

"The queen is very lovely," he said. "I was honored to meet her."

"I'm only interested in your medical opinion," Lydia answered sharply. "What's her condition?"

"She's in excellent health, but I don't suppose that's our primary concern," he said dryly. "You want to know why she can't have children."

"It's true, then!" Lydia's voice vibrated with triumph.

"Not exactly. She needs a little minor corrective surgery. After that she can have as many children as she likes."

Lydia's disappointment was hard to swallow. "Can you guarantee that?"

"I'll stake my reputation on it—my *medical* reputation," he stressed before she could reply.

Lydia rallied quickly. "That's not what you're going to tell Stephanie. You're going to tell her she can never have children."

"Are you out of your mind? Why would I do that?"

"Because I'm instructing you to," Lydia answered steadily.

"It's out of the question. I let you blackmail me into giving you the results of my examination, but you can't make me do this."

"Aren't your scruples a little late?"

"What I did was unethical, but harmless. You're asking me to commit an act that could be considered treasonous, not to mention the anguish it would cause that poor woman. She wants a child. The whole succession to the throne depends on her having one."

"The monarchy will survive."

"You damn well bet it will," he answered grimly.

"I admire your concern for your country, especiall[
since you'll be an expatriate if you try to cross me."

"That's an empty threat. You can't make it stick.
necessary, I'll tell the queen what you asked me to do."

"Which one of us do you think she'll believe after I te[
her about your affair with a married noblewoman? Do[
that show integrity?"

He sighed. "That was a long time ago, and it wasn't [
sordid as you make it sound. We were in love. I wanted t
marry her."

"You men think with your loins," Lydia said contemp[
tuously. "Did you really expect her to leave a baron fo[
you?"

He ran a hand wearily over his face. "It doesn't matte[
now. It's over and done with."

"Her husband might think differently. The medic[
board, too, if they knew about the abortion you pe[
formed on your paramour."

"What could I do? I begged her not to, but she threa[
ened to go to some back-room butcher if I didn't take ca[
of her myself. How do you think I felt? My own child, fo[
God's sake!"

"That won't get you any sympathy," Lydia answere[
crisply. "How many patients do you think you'd have i
the story got out?"

"Don't you have an ounce of compassion in you[
makeup?" he pleaded.

"When I can afford it. Right now I can't. Are you goin[
to cooperate?"

It was dark out, but Stephanie hadn't lit the lamps. Sh[
was standing at one of the windows in her sitting room
staring out at the stars. Pepe was a darker smudge at he[
feet. She didn't move when she heard Morgan calling he[

Pepe betrayed her presence when Morgan appeared in the doorway. The dog ran to him, barking a greeting.

"Stephanie? Are you in here?" He snapped on the lights. When she turned, blinking in the sudden brightness, Morgan looked at her closely. "What's wrong, angel?"

"Sit down, Morgan, we have to talk," she said tonelessly.

He paled. "What is it? Are you ill?"

"In a way."

She told him what the doctor had told her, speaking in an emotionless voice that didn't fool him for an instant. He let her tell the whole story without interrupting, then he took her in his arms.

"I'm so sorry, darling," he murmured, stroking her hair gently.

"Yes, I am too," she answered stoically.

"You don't have to be so damn brave. Go ahead and cry. It might make you feel better."

"I would if it would do any good, but it won't. Nothing will." She drew out of his arms. "You can start the divorce proceedings. I'll leave as soon as possible."

He stared at her incredulously. "What are you talking about?"

"You need an heir, and I can't give you one," she said patiently. "I understand that."

"Then maybe you can explain it to me. I married the woman I love, not a baby factory. I'm disappointed that we won't have children, but that's not the most important thing in the world. You are."

"You have an obligation to your country."

"I have an obligation to be the best ruler I can be, not to give up the love of my life."

Stephanie shook her head. "How long do you think it would be before you started to feel cheated?"

"Maybe in fifty or sixty years, but by then I'll be too old for fatherhood anyway." He tried to bring a smile to her face.

Her expression didn't lighten. "Do you think the people would accept a barren queen?"

"You've won their hearts in the short time you've been here. I don't believe they'd turn against you, but if that ever happened, I'd abdicate."

Her protective shell showed the first signs of cracking. "You couldn't do that!" she gasped.

"I could, and I would." He gathered her in his arms and held her tightly. "What does it take to convince you that you're the focal point of my life? You're as necessary to me as breathing. I've told you over and over again that I'll never let you go. When are you going to start believing it?"

The tears came then. All her pent-up grief and disappointment came pouring out, leaving room for hope. She'd steeled herself against losing Morgan, and that had been the most crushing blow of all. His passionate assurances brought balm to her troubled soul.

They were closer than ever that night. Morgan held her in his arms and told her in every way he knew how that she was the center of his universe. Stephanie finally allowed herself to believe him because she wanted to so desperately. But a shadow had fallen across their perfect romance.

Lydia was waiting for her when she came downstairs the next morning. "How did you like Dr. Courbet?" she asked. "He's our most eminent gynecologist."

"He was very nice," Stephanie answered noncommittally.

"I'll bet he told you that you had nothing to worry about, didn't he?"

"He said I was slightly rundown. I...uh...I need to take some iron pills."

Morgan had urged her not to make a public announcement. He said it was no one's business but their own. When she tentatively mentioned the people's right to know, he said the time to answer questions was when they were asked.

Lydia was regarding her narrowly. "No major problems, then?"

"Did you think there would be?" Stephanie didn't want to tell an outright lie, so evasion seemed the best course.

"Certainly not," Lydia answered hastily. "I just wanted to be sure you liked the doctor I recommended."

Stephanie tried hard to be the normal, happy person she'd always been, but it was difficult. Her self-confidence had suffered a setback. Morgan went out of his way to shower attention on her, which made it worse in a way. He was almost too gentle. She didn't want love through pity.

When she grew thinner and more taut, Lydia approached Morgan discreetly. "I think Stephanie is overdoing her outside activities," she said. "She needs to have some fun. What would you think about having a party here in the castle?"

"That sounds like a wonderful idea," he said gratefully.

"Let's make it a real gala. Maybe a masked ball," Lydia suggested. "We'll invite all our old friends. Stephanie should start to have more of a social life."

"That might be just what she needs right now," Morgan said thoughtfully.

"I'll take care of everything, and I'll get her involved."

"I really appreciate that, Lydia."

"It will be my pleasure, believe me," she replied.

Stephanie suspected that the party was being given for her benefit. She was touched by Lydia's concern, as well as Morgan's. In appreciation of their thoughtfulness she took an active part in the planning.

She and Lydia discussed food, decorations and costumes, making long lists of things to do. After her initial pretense of interest, Stephanie found she was actually enjoying herself. It was a relief to think about something other than her troubles for a change.

"Have you decided on a costume yet?" Lydia asked at one of their many meetings.

"I thought I'd go as a clown," Stephanie said. "One of the ones with a big happy smile painted on." That would symbolize her new attitude.

"What fun! You can wear a curly wig and a big red nose. No one will ever recognize you, even without a mask."

Stephanie glanced at the first few names on the long guest list. "I won't know any of these people with or without their masks."

"Sure you will." Lydia took the list away from her. "You know Sara Plechette and her cousin, Amanda. You had them here for lunch with their children."

"Oh, yes, they're charming. Who else will I know?"

"More people than you imagine. What's Phillipe going to wear?"

"He's going as Zorro, in black pants and shirt and a big plumed hat."

"Sounds like one of the three musketeers," Lydia commented.

"No, they wore knee breeches and satin coats. I couldn't coax him into anything like that."

"Men." Lydia nodded in understanding. "They have to look macho."

Stephanie's expression was suddenly doubtful. "Maybe I should wear something more glamorous."

"Not at all. Stick by your choice. I'm not wearing anything frivolous. I'm going as Napoleon."

Stephanie laughed. "Don't tell me Henri will be your Josephine?"

"Don't be ridiculous," Lydia said sharply. "He'll be a troubadour."

It was interesting the way they'd chosen costumes that mirrored their personalities, Stephanie reflected. Including herself. Pagliacci hid his sorrow under a clown's makeup. She banished the thought as soon as it surfaced. There would be no more sad songs for her. From now on she was going to concentrate on her blessings.

Morgan was opening a bottle of champagne when Stephanie came out of the shower on the night of the costume ball. His gala mood wasn't solely due to the party. Morgan had watched with increasing relief as Stephanie shook off her depression.

After a couple of sips, she set her glass down. "I'd better get started on my makeup."

"There's no hurry."

Before she could stop him, he pulled out the tucked-in ends of the towel she'd wrapped around herself. As it slipped to the floor he took her in his arms, parting the short robe he wore so their nude bodies were joined.

His masculinity was very seductive. Stephanie allowed herself several moments to enjoy the heat and firmness of his body before reluctantly drawing away.

"In case you've forgotten, we have a number of guests due to arrive shortly," she said.

"They can wait," he growled, trying to pull her back into his arms.

"We have to get dressed. After the party I'll give you my full attention," she promised.

"I might not be in the mood then."

She laughed confidently. "I'll take my chances."

"Okay, but you never can tell," he warned.

Stephanie had just finished stuffing her long hair under a bright orange wig when Morgan came into the dressing room. She'd painted her face white and drawn exaggerated black eyelashes on her lids. A wide, curving band of red gave her a permanent smile. When she turned to show Morgan the result, her eyes widened in admiration.

The tight black pants molded closely to his lean hips, and the partially buttoned shirt revealed a glimpse of the crisp hair on his broad chest. A plumed hat sat rakishly on his dark head, and he flourished a long, slender sword.

"Well, what do you think?" His eyes were a blue gleam behind the black mask.

"I think you'll need that sword to fight off the women."

"What makes you sure I want to?" he joked. "You had your chance and you turned me down."

"Only temporarily."

"That's no excuse. It would serve you right if some other woman got me on the rebound."

They bantered back and forth while she got into her shapeless clown suit. "How do I look?" she asked, adjusting the voluminous folds.

"Hilarious. Any circus would snap you up in a minute."

"That's not one of your better compliments. It's a little late to think of it, but I wish I'd chosen to be Cleopatra."

"I like you better this way," he said fondly. "All the men would have made a play for you, and I'd have been jealous."

"I guess you won't have anything to worry about tonight," she said ruefully.

The first guests were arriving as they went downstairs, and Stephanie and Morgan were soon separated. The trickle of couples turned into a steady stream until all the large rooms were crowded.

Two orchestras playing different kinds of music were positioned in separate drawing rooms, and a space had been cleared for dancing in each room. The sound of laughing voices mingled with the music, creating a party atmosphere that was heightened by the colorful costumes of the guests.

Pirates danced with shepherdesses, while Roman senators in togas discussed the stock market with hoboes. Stephanie managed to recognize a few people she knew, but most of the costumes were effective disguises. Only Morgan was recognizable to everyone.

Stephanie was talking to a caveman when another person dressed as a clown approached her.

"We have a lot in common," he said in a voice that told her he was male. "The question is, how *much* in common? If I asked you to dance, would you be offended?"

She laughed. "Not unless you stepped on my feet."

"That's a relief. I was afraid you might take a swing at me."

"You could have played it safe by asking a mermaid to dance."

"You're more my type. I like women who aren't afraid to look comical."

She was gathering enough left-handed compliments to last a lifetime, Stephanie reflected. "Maybe I look even funnier under this makeup," she said.

"That's okay, so do I," he said, leading her onto the dance floor.

They joked together easily, moving slowly around the crowded floor. Suddenly Stephanie caught sight of Morgan dancing with a woman in a ballerina costume. The brief tutu showed off her long legs to great advantage, and the low-cut bodice displayed her breasts admirably. She had flowing dark hair that curled around her ivory shoulders. The woman was not only gorgeous, she was definitely interested in Morgan—and he wasn't exactly indifferent to her. They seemed unaware of the people around them as they danced closely.

"Who is that woman dancing with Mor...with Phillipe?" Stephanie corrected herself. "If you can guess, that is. She looks familiar."

"That's Alicia LeBec. No one could mistake that gorgeous body." His voice held male appreciation.

"Oh, right. I thought I recognized her." Stephanie was careful to keep her own voice casual.

"It looks as though they're renewing old acquaintances, doesn't it? I suppose you never get a woman like Alicia out of your system."

"Even after you're married?" Stephanie asked evenly.

He laughed. "What does duty have to do with romance?"

"You think Phillipe married out of a sense of duty?"

Her partner became belatedly cautious. "I'm sure that wasn't the case. The queen is a beautiful woman. But he and Alicia had quite a thing going between them. It certainly wasn't a secret."

"So I've heard," Stephanie murmured.

"You didn't know about it?"

"Well, I . . . I was out of the country."

"Ah, that explains it, although it went on for some time. A lot of people expected them to get married. I've always wondered what happened."

"Maybe they discovered they weren't really in love with each other," Stephanie said curtly.

"They seem to be having second thoughts, don't they?"

"If you'll excuse me, I have to see someone." Stephanie left him abruptly. She was grateful for the painted-on clown smile when Lydia waylaid her.

"Isn't it a fabulous party?" she asked.

"That's not the word for it," Stephanie answered.

"Have you been meeting a lot of people?" Lydia asked. "Isn't it delicious when they don't know who you are?"

"You do find out things."

"I'll bet there will be some red faces when the masks come off at midnight," Lydia predicted.

"No doubt. I'll see you later. I have to go touch up my makeup." Stephanie was anxious to get away. She didn't get very far, though, before Morgan stopped her.

"You and Lydia did a terrific job, angel." He was smiling. "Everyone is having a great time. The masks were an inspired idea."

"You don't seem to have any trouble recognizing your old friends," she said grimly.

"No, but I have an advantage. I know them so well."

"Some exceedingly well, would you say?"

He frowned slightly. "What does that mean?"

"Nothing. I guess I'm just feeling like a bit of an outsider."

"That's nonsense. This is your party."

A blonde dressed as a harem girl came up and took Morgan's arm. "I've been waiting for a chance at you all night," she cooed. "Come and dance with me."

With an amused smile in Stephanie's direction, he allowed himself to be carried off.

What else could he do? she asked herself reasonably, stifling her disappointment. They'd had hardly a word together all evening. She'd predicted this would happen, but her pleasure in the party dimmed. It wouldn't be over soon, either. They'd planned a midnight supper, which was bound to drag on with so many people to be served. The guests couldn't even be counted on to leave shortly afterward. Everybody was having such a good time.

At ten minutes to twelve, one of the orchestras drew attention with a drumroll. Lydia waited by the microphone until all the merrymakers crowded around.

"Before the unmasking at midnight, each lady gets to choose a supper partner," she announced. "All selections are final. There will be no exchanges if you regret your choice after you get a good look at him," she instructed to general laughter.

Stephanie frowned in annoyance. This wasn't part of their plans. She started toward Lydia amidst the general hilarity. Women were pretending to squabble over the handsomer men.

"We never discussed this," she said when she reached her sister-in-law.

"I know. It just came to me. Isn't it a howl?" Lydia grinned as she watched the activity swirling around them. "They're really letting their hair down."

"A regular laugh a minute," Stephanie commented acidly.

Lydia stared at her wide-eyed. "You don't object, do you?"

"I think it's juvenile. What do you have planned next? Spin the bottle?"

"Oh, Stephanie, lighten up. It's all innocent fun. Go find Phillipe if you don't want to switch partners."

Stephanie didn't even bother to look for him. She had no hope that Morgan would remain unchosen. As she was standing where Lydia had left her, fuming, her former partner, the clown, approached.

"I've been saving myself for you," he said.

"You mean no one picked you?"

"How did you guess?" He chuckled. "Looks like you struck out, too. Well, never mind. We'll console each other."

"I can't understand why you weren't snapped up," she commented ironically. "You're so sensitive."

Lydia appeared at the microphone again. "I hope you've all found your partners because it's the witching hour, time to unmask. If you should find yourself with someone you don't know, count your blessings. You've made a new friend."

"This is it." Stephanie's partner reached for his mask. "I hope you won't be too shocked."

"Not nearly as much as you're going to be," she answered sweetly.

Her auburn hair came tumbling down as she pulled off the curly wig. After that she removed her mask and the red plastic nose. The clown makeup still distorted her face, however.

He stared at her, puzzled by some faint familiarity. "Have we met?"

"Allow me to introduce myself. I'm Stephanie Morgantrelle."

His painful flush was evident even under the white greasepaint. "I didn't . . . I hope you don't . . ." He swallowed hard and tried again. "If I said anything disrespectful I hope you'll forgive me. I had no idea who you were."

"I'm sure you didn't," she answered evenly.

His wild scrambling to recall what he'd said was almost visible. The horrified expression on his face intensified as he remembered their conversation on the dance floor.

"I just like to joke around a lot—you know, tell wild stories about people. None of them are true," he assured her earnestly.

"If that's your idea of fun, how do I know you're telling the truth now?"

"I wouldn't lie to *you*."

"That's very comforting." Stephanie was suddenly tired of the man. "I must see to my other guests. Why don't you get something to eat? Or perhaps you'd prefer a drink," she said mockingly.

Leaving him standing there, shaken, she went upstairs to remove her makeup. She used cold cream first, then washed her face with soap and water until her skin glowed with its normal color.

She was tempted to remain in her room. Would anyone really miss her? Banishing the self-pitying thought, she applied lipstick and a touch of mascara. This was her party. Besides, she'd left something downstairs—her husband. Anyone who thought he was the door prize was badly mistaken!

Most of the guests were seated at small tables that had been set up wherever there was space. The overflow sat on couches, balancing their plates on their laps.

Stephanie drifted from one group to another, hearing enthusiastic comments on what a wonderful party it was. Her gracious replies were a little abstracted. She was looking for Morgan.

She finally found him at a table for two in a corner. He was sharing it with Alicia, which wasn't a big surprise. Stephanie's determined smile felt wooden as she greeted them.

"There you are, darling," Morgan exclaimed. "I was wondering what happened to you."

"Were you looking for me?" she asked, trying to make the question sound innocent.

"We both were. You know Alicia LeBec." He turned to include the other woman.

Stephanie nodded. "We've met."

"I love your costume." Alicia smiled. "I never would have known who you were."

"A lot of people had that trouble," Stephanie answered.

"What happened to your funny face?" Morgan asked.

"I washed it off. Nobody flirts with a clown in a red nose," she answered lightly.

"I thought you looked cute." He chuckled.

A waiter appeared with a silver tray holding stemmed glasses filled with white wine. Morgan handed one to Stephanie, then served Alicia and took one himself.

"Have you had anything to eat?" he asked Stephanie. "I'll be happy to fix a plate for you."

"Yes, do join us," Alicia urged.

"No, thanks, I'm not hungry," Stephanie declined. "But don't let me stop you. I have to finish my hostess duties." She moved away in spite of Morgan's objections.

It sometimes seemed as though the party would never end. After supper a group of men gathered around the piano to sing barbershop quartet songs. Their voices weren't bad, but they appeared excruciatingly funny to everyone because of their incongruous costumes.

The act was such a success that other guests wanted to perform, and an impromptu talent show developed. It was almost three in the morning when a few of the less hardy souls departed. Another full hour went by before everyone else cleared out.

Morgan sat down on the foot of the bed to take off his shoes. "You can be proud of yourself, angel. That was one smashing party."

She continued to brush her long hair. "I'm glad you enjoyed it."

He looked up at an indefinable note in her voice. "Didn't you?"

"Oh, sure. But it wasn't a reunion for me like it was for you. I mean getting together with your old friends," she added hastily.

"That was fun," he acknowledged. "I'm glad you got to meet them. We'll have to do it more often."

"We haven't done much that was purely social," Stephanie said slowly. "I didn't realize you'd missed it."

"I haven't. I was thinking of you. All work and no play..."

"Makes Jane a dull girl," she finished soberly.

He came over to plant a kiss on top of her head. "You'll never be that."

She watched in the mirror as he took off his shirt and then his trousers. "How did you happen to wind up with Alicia for your supper partner? I imagine several women ran a footrace to get to you."

He smiled indulgently. "That's nothing to get puffed up about. They knew who I was. It's polite to make a fuss over the host."

That didn't answer her question, but Stephanie didn't like to ask it again—directly. "Alicia is a stunning woman," she remarked casually.

"She never seems to change, and she's older than you are."

"That *does* make her ancient." Stephanie's mouth thinned ominously.

Morgan laughed. "That wasn't a very gallant remark, was it?"

"It wouldn't get applause from either one of us."

"I meant it as a compliment to both of you." His eyes suddenly sparkled mischievously. "I *like* older women."

Stephanie didn't share his amusement. "Your use of the plural is revealing," she said coldly.

"You know I was only joking." He stretched luxuriously. "Come to bed, love of my life. The sun will be up soon."

As she watched the muscles rippling in his splendidly nude body, Stephanie felt her tension drain away. Why was she trying to pick an argument? Morgan was here with *her*, wasn't he?

She turned out the lights and slid into bed, moving close to him. When he stroked her hair languidly she kissed his throat.

"Mmm, that's nice," he murmured contentedly.

After waiting a moment she trailed her fingers down his chest to the flat plane of his stomach. His hand closed around hers, preventing her from going any farther.

"I'm really zonked, angel. Do you mind?" he asked.

"No, I...I understand," she said after an instant of surprise.

"I told you to take advantage of me while I was in the mood," he teased drowsily.

Morgan fell asleep only moments later, but Stephanie stared into the darkness, unable to follow his example. This was the first time he had ever rejected her.

She told herself it was perfectly understandable. They'd both had a long night. It was no big deal. But the small chill that traveled up her spine refused to go away.

Chapter Ten

After the masquerade party Stephanie's life became more hectic. Invitations to social events poured in, formal ones on engraved squares, handwritten notes, phone calls. These were in addition to the usual requests for their presence at state functions. There wouldn't have been enough days in the week to accept them all.

When Stephanie mentioned this to Morgan, he said, "We'll cut back on the public appearances. People are making too many demands on you."

"I don't mind," she assured him.

"You've been wonderful about it, angel, but you deserve a private life, too."

She thought wistfully of the quiet days they had spent together when they were newly married, riding with the dogs and having intimate dinners alone. But no honeymoon lasted forever. It was natural for Morgan to want to see his friends.

She tried not to sigh. "Well, you'd better tell me which of these invitations to accept."

"It's up to you."

"I don't even know half the people."

He looked at her narrowly. "Don't you want to accept them, Stephanie?"

"Oh, sure," she answered brightly. "I was giving you the choice because you know which ones are most apt to be fun."

His watchful expression relaxed. "Let me take a look at our options."

Their nights were soon filled with a round of dinners and parties that ranged from simple to elaborate. Some of the faces at the larger affairs remained only vaguely familiar, but a small, elite group was always present. Lady Alicia LeBec was one of them.

Stephanie tried not to let it bother her. She certainly couldn't fault either Morgan or Alicia for their behavior. No hint of their former relationship was evident. They joked easily together like old friends. If Stephanie sometimes felt a pang at their shared remembrances, she tried to remind herself that it was only normal for them to refer to past experiences. She would undoubtedly do the same thing with *her* old friends.

Morgan appeared to thrive on all the activity, but Stephanie didn't possess his energy. Sometimes after a busy day filled with committee meetings and appointments, she yearned for a quiet evening at home. Since Morgan didn't seem to share her preference, she didn't mention it.

There were a lot of things they didn't mention anymore. The discovery that she couldn't bear children had brought about a subtle change in their marriage. They were suddenly very careful of what they said to each other. Even their lovemaking had a hint of desperation sometimes.

They both tried so hard to give pleasure, as though to compensate.

The strain was beginning to wear Stephanie down. At a swimming party on a Sunday afternoon at the end of summer, she almost fell asleep on a chaise. They'd had a gourmet lunch around the pool, complete with wine, which always made her sleepy when she drank it in the afternoon. The soothing effect of glittering blue water, sun and Chablis made her eyelids droop.

"Stephanie is falling asleep on us," their host observed. Vincent Cantrelle was a man Alicia dated often.

"You fed me too well." Stephanie opened her eyes and smiled.

"She's right." Morgan patted his flat stomach. "A few more lunches like that and I'll have to go on a diet."

"You'll work it off in the pool," Vincent said. "That's how I keep my weight down. I swim every morning. It's a lot more fun than dieting."

"That would be good for you, too, Phillipe," Lydia said. "Why don't we put in a pool?"

"Why should I go to all that trouble when I can use Vincent's?" Morgan grinned.

"No, really, I'm serious," Lydia persisted. "We have the perfect spot out by the gazebo."

"It might not be a bad idea," Henri commented.

Morgan looked at Stephanie. "Would you like to have a swimming pool?"

"It would be nice," she answered.

"All right, we'll build one."

"How's that for a doting husband?" Vincent asked.

"King Louis didn't do more for Marie Antionette," Henri agreed.

"Don't put me in her class," Stephanie protested. "I was thinking how wonderful it would be for the children at the hospital. Swimming is great therapy. We could bring them over several times a week."

"Oh, Stephanie, don't you ever think of anything but children?" Lydia exclaimed impatiently.

Stephanie flushed as everyone glanced unconsciously at her slim figure. They quickly masked their speculation, but it was painfully obvious to her.

"My wife is a very compassionate woman," Morgan answered for her.

The subject was changed swiftly, but Stephanie couldn't force herself to join in. After a few moments she stood up and murmured some vague excuse.

Morgan followed her across the broad lawn. When he caught up with her, he put his arm around her waist and led her to the grape arbor in the distance. The leafy arch provided a measure of privacy. He kissed her in the sun-dappled shade.

"What are we doing here when we could be home making love?" he asked softly.

She wasn't diverted. "I'm all right, Morgan. I just wanted to get out of the sun for a few minutes. Go on back, I'll join you shortly."

"It was simply an unfortunate remark," he said gently. "Lydia couldn't have any way of knowing."

"I realize that."

"You have to stop torturing yourself, darling."

"I'm not. I've accepted the fact."

He stared at her broodingly. "I wish there were something I could do."

"It isn't your fault, it's mine," she answered tautly. The expression on his face made her ashamed. "I'm sorry! I know it's as bad for you as it is for me."

He held her close. "Nothing is bad as long as we have each other."

That was what worried her. How long would she be enough for Morgan?

"Love me, darling." That was as close as she could get to telling him her innermost fears.

"I always will," he promised in a voice husky with emotion.

Stephanie decided that maybe Lydia was right. Perhaps she was too involved with children. The volunteer bureau was running smoothly, and she was proud of what she'd accomplished. But now it was time to move on to something else.

She approached Morgan with her new idea. "Could I go with you when you open the fall session of the World Trade Congress?"

"Certainly, if you think you'd be interested."

"What exactly is its function?"

"The board tries to find ways to sell our products in foreign countries, for one thing. That involves surveys on comparable prices of competitors, and investigating possible markets. Then we have to woo the customers. I suppose you could call it running a global department store."

She smiled. "Do we have markdown sales?"

"Not if we can help it, although it's the one thing we haven't tried. You might suggest it."

Stephanie simply listened and learned at the opening session, finding it extremely interesting. Morgan was right about the department-store concept. They had a variety of things to sell. The problem was attracting customers.

Morgan's function in opening the session was largely ceremonial. He wasn't required to attend after that, but Stephanie went to all the meetings. Her stimulating days made up in part for her boring nights. How Morgan put up with them was beyond her.

Was it because of Alicia? Stephanie didn't want to think
that way, but ever since the woman had come back into his
life he'd changed. It couldn't be the parties he looked for
ward to—they were all alike. It was becoming increas
ingly difficult to pretend to be enjoying herself, especiall
when Morgan took to disappearing for longish periods o
time. One evening he went into the garden alone—and re
turned with Alicia.

"Are you trying to start gossip?" Lydia asked play
fully.

Morgan frowned. "If anyone can make something ou
of two people wanting a breath of fresh air, they must b
pretty hard up."

"It's awfully warm in here," Alicia said. "Summer'
last gasp, I suppose."

Vincent joined them. "Where have you been with my
date? In case you've forgotten, you're a married mar
now."

"Thank you for reminding me," Morgan said icily be
fore stalking off.

Stephanie turned away hastily so he wouldn't know
she'd witnessed the little exchange. He was testy all eve
ning, not at all his usual urbane self. Had he and Alicia
argued? If so, they made up speedily.

Stephanie glimpsed them standing together in the well of
a stairway, partially hidden by a large plant. Morgan was
talking and gesturing angrily, while Alicia listened pa
tiently. When he'd finished, she put her hand on his arm
and said something that placated him. After a moment he
smiled wryly and squeezed her hand. Stephanie walked
away. She didn't want to see any more.

They left earlier than usual that night.

Stephanie had promised herself she wouldn't mention
Alicia's name, but she couldn't help herself. When they

were getting ready for bed she asked casually, "Where did you disappear to this evening?"

"I'd scarcely call it a disappearance to go outside to cool off." Morgan pulled off his tie with unnecessary vigor.

She ignored the warning sign. "I guess it *was* warm. Alicia was complaining about it, also."

"Not you, too!" he said explosively. "Why is everyone making a big deal about Alicia and me all of a sudden?"

"I merely remarked that she found it stuffy in the drawing room."

"In more ways than one," he muttered.

Stephanie's temper started to rise. She'd put up with these boring events for his sake. "Every night isn't New Year's Eve," she remarked evenly. "The rest of us managed to put up with it without being rude."

"What you're really saying is that I was indiscreet."

She felt sick inside, but she managed to keep her voice steady. "That depends on what you were doing in the garden."

"Do you honestly think I was making mad, passionate love to Alicia where any one of fifty guests could stroll by and see us?" he demanded.

"I would hope you'd use more discretion."

Incredulity replaced anger as he stared at her taut posture and pale face. "You *are* wondering if that's what happened."

She turned away. "We're both tired. Let's not discuss it anymore."

He pulled her back to face him. "We damn well *better* discuss it! If you think I'm having an affair with another woman, there's something seriously wrong with our marriage."

Stephanie drew in her breath sharply. "I didn't say that."

"You didn't have to. It's written all over you. This goes deeper than my leaving a boring party for a half hour."

"With Alicia," she reminded him.

"It wasn't planned," he answered impatiently.

"Maybe not, but she's always there." Stephanie's frustration boiled over. "Wherever we go."

"She's part of the group." Morgan raked his fingers through his hair in his own gesture of frustration. "You wanted to go to these things."

"Are you kidding?" She looked at him in astonishment. "I only go because *you* want to."

They stared at each other for a moment before he broke into laughter. "I do believe we've set a record for misunderstandings. I'm fed up with endless parties." His laughter died as he took her in his arms. "You were so unhappy after you found out about having a baby. I thought you needed to get out more."

"And I thought you were getting bored with me."

"How could I be when I never know what you're going to come up with next?" he teased gently. "Your mysterious mind makes our marriage as exciting as your heavenly body."

"That isn't any mystery to you," she murmured.

"It always seems to be. Each time is new and different."

His fevered kiss dissolved the hard core of misery in her chest. They clung together, moving in mute invitation. Morgan prolonged the exquisite moment until their passion was a throbbing ache.

When she whispered his name over and over again, he led her to the bed. She quivered as he undressed her slowly, pausing to cover her breasts with kisses before he removed her skirt. His avid gaze devoured her body, clad

nly in sheer panty hose, sending a ripple of excitement
rough her.

His caresses were more erotic, veiled by the sheer ny-
on. When she arched her body and uttered tiny cries of
elight, he removed his own clothing without taking his
yes off her.

She watched breathlessly. His deliberation was almost
nbearable. Liquid fire raced through her veins as his body
as revealed in all its male power. She was taut with de-
ire when he finally drew her close for the ultimate em-
race.

Their union was both passionate and sweet, a reaffir-
ation of a mutual love that was stronger than any mis-
nderstanding. The peaceful aftermath was filled with
hared contentment.

Morgan stroked her hair lovingly. "I'm sorry I was such
bear tonight."

"Don't be. It cleared the air."

"I still can't believe you thought I was having an affair
ith Alicia."

"I didn't really, but I knew something was wrong. You
ept slipping away and I didn't know why."

"It was the only way I could get through the evening."

"Well, that's all over. From now on, the Morgantrelles
end their regrets."

"You have a slight tendency to go overboard." Morgan
miled. "We don't have to become hermits. A little mod-
ration is called for, that's all."

"Whatever you say." She wriggled happily in his arms.

Stephanie's life couldn't have been more idyllic from
hen on. The nights were sheer heaven, and her days were
ngrossing. She'd developed such an interest in the World

Trade Congress that the president of the board had ap
pointed her to an important committee.

It wasn't a token gesture, either. The long hours she pu
in attending meetings and writing up reports had earne
her the job. People valued her opinion, which was ver
gratifying. She knew their respect was for her ability, no
her rank.

One person who wasn't happy with her new life-styl
was Lydia. "How can you just drop out of everything fo
no good reason?" she asked.

"We haven't dropped out, we've just cut back," Steph
anie explained.

"But why? We were having such fun."

"Maybe some of us were," Stephanie answered dryly.

Lydia gazed at her obliquely. "You shouldn't let Phi
lipe's friendship with Alicia bother you. Old flames ar
rarely rekindled."

Stephanie raised an eyebrow. "Rarely?"

"That didn't come out right," Lydia said hastily. "
meant they've settled for being good friends."

"I know," Stephanie answered confidently as she move
toward the stairs. "If you'll excuse me, I have some phon
calls to make."

Lydia didn't give up easily. She kept trying to coa
Stephanie to go everywhere she and Henri went. Steph
anie couldn't really understand why her sister-in-law ha
become so dependent on them all of a sudden. It was nic
that they'd achieved a pleasant relationship, but she wa
overdoing a good thing.

"It's so dull around here with you and Phillipe awa
every day," Lydia complained one afternoon when Steph
anie returned home.

Stephanie sighed. She was tired, and all she wanted to do was take a nice, relaxing bath. "We're not gone every day. At least Morgan isn't."

"Maybe not the complete day, but he leaves right after you do. Where does he go for several hours every morning?"

"I don't know. Why don't you ask him?"

Lydia appeared horrified. "Please don't tell him I mentioned it! I wasn't spying, honestly."

Stephanie looked at her curiously. "Why would I think a thing like that?"

"Phillipe might. We didn't always get along this well, and I'd hate to spoil things. Please don't make him annoyed with me."

"That's the last thing I'd want to do. Stop worrying over nothing," Stephanie said impatiently.

"I will if you promise not to tell him," Lydia insisted.

"Okay, I promise. Now can I go take a bath?"

The balmy weather changed to rain with the advent of autumn. Several people Stephanie worked with came down with colds, so it was perhaps inevitable for her to catch one, too.

She returned home one afternoon with a scratchy throat and a stuffed-up head. Morgan took one look at her and told her to get into bed.

"I can't." She sighed. "We have that dinner dance to go to."

"You're going to have your dinner in bed," he stated firmly.

"It's only a cold." Her protest was halfhearted.

"Colds can turn into something more serious if you don't take care of them."

She allowed herself to be persuaded, since the idea of getting dressed and making polite conversation for hours was less than appealing.

Lydia didn't take the news well when she phoned a few minutes later to ask what Stephanie was wearing. "You can't disappoint Marian," she exclaimed. "The party is in your honor."

"Morgan won't let me go."

"Then *he* has to. It would be a direct insult if neither of you showed up."

"Absolutely not," Morgan said when Stephanie relayed the message.

"Maybe you should go. We haven't been out in over a week, and there's no sense in staying here and watching me sleep."

"I like to watch you sleep. You look like a little kitten, all curled up with your head on my shoulder."

"Actually, I should go in the other bedroom tonight so you don't catch my germs."

"No way," he declared. "The day we sleep apart is the day our marriage is in trouble."

She smiled at his vehemence. "Shouldn't that be the *night* we sleep apart?"

"Day or night, it's not going to happen."

Stephanie gave in easily on that point, and Morgan reluctantly allowed himself to be coaxed into going to the party without her. Neither thought the event was that important, but Lydia was so insistent that it was easier to give in to her.

"You look so handsome I'm having second thoughts about letting you go out alone," Stephanie remarked when Morgan was dressed and ready to leave. He was especially elegant in a well-tailored dinner jacket.

"I won't be alone, I'll be surrounded by a bevy of adoring females," he teased.

"That's what I'm afraid of."

"You were the one who said I should go," he pointed out.

"But I didn't say you had to enjoy yourself."

"I never do without you." He leaned down to kiss the top of her head.

Stephanie slept fitfully because of her stuffy head. She awoke when Morgan slid into bed next to her.

"What time is it?" she mumbled.

"Shh, go back to sleep," he answered gently.

She opened her eyes to look at the clock on the nightstand. Its luminous face read two o'clock. She sniffled and went back to sleep.

Morgan was gone when she awoke the next morning late because of her restless night. She didn't have to be told to stay in bed; she felt rotten.

Lydia's visit later in the morning wasn't exactly welcome, but Stephanie tried to appear interested in her account of the previous night's party. She knew her sister-in-law meant well.

"Everyone felt terrible that you weren't there," Lydia said.

"I was sorry, too," Stephanie replied insincerely.

"It's a shame. You missed a truly fun evening. If Phillipe enjoyed himself you *know* it was a success. Aren't men the limit? You have to coax them to go, and then they don't want to leave."

Stephanie suddenly remembered looking at the clock. "I'm glad he had a good time."

Lydia laughed. "I guess you could safely say that. I think he danced every dance."

"That's nice." Stephanie wondered if Lydia was going to stay all day.

"Where did he learn to do the Charleston?"

"I have no idea," Stephanie said wearily.

"He and Alicia looked like professionals. Everybody cleared the floor and watched them. They must have practiced together to be that smooth."

Stephanie's attention sharpened, but she kept her voice casual. "I suppose they're both good dancers."

"That's probably it, but none of the rest of us could get the hang of it."

After chattering on for another half hour, Lydia finally left her alone.

Stephanie's relief was tempered by a vague uneasiness she tried to suppress. There was nothing portentous in the fact that Morgan had danced with Alicia, she told herself. Naturally he would. But how *did* they perform so well together?

Half-remembered things kept coming back to Stephanie. Lydia's inadvertent disclosure that Morgan went out regularly every morning. Where did he go, and why hadn't he mentioned the fact?

Stephanie was immediately ashamed of her suspicions. Hadn't they settled the whole subject of Alicia? Every aspect of their marriage was perfect now. Morgan would have no reason to be unfaithful. He was a wonderful husband, and she was the luckiest woman in the world.

Morgan came to visit her a short time later. "How are you feeling, angel?"

"I've felt better," she admitted.

He looked concerned. "Maybe I should call the doctor."

"I'm not really sick, I just want sympathy." She smiled.

"How about some tea to go with it? Have you had anything to eat?"

"I'm not hungry."

"You should eat something," he urged.

"Perhaps later. Have you had lunch?"

"No, I just got back."

When he didn't elaborate, Stephanie said casually, "You must have gotten out early. I didn't even hear you get up this morning."

"I tried not to wake you."

"That was very thoughtful." After a slight pause she said, "Did you have a nice time last night?"

"Better than I expected."

"Oh? Because of all the adoring females?"

"They were part of it." He laughed.

"Lydia said you were the life of the party."

He made a wry face. "That always conjures up images of people prancing around with lamp shades on their heads."

"I can't conceive of you doing a thing like that."

"I certainly hope not!"

"You're full of surprises, though," she remarked lightly. "I always thought you avoided the spotlight."

He looked suddenly wary. "I presume you're referring to the dance I did with Alicia."

"Lydia asked me where you learned to do the Charleston, and I told her I had no idea."

"It's an outdated American dance. Nobody there last night would have known whether we did it right or not."

"You must have faked it quite well."

He frowned in annoyance. "I didn't know you meant it when you told me not to enjoy myself."

Stephanie tried to deflect the quarrel she could sense building. "I was only joking."

He wasn't appeased. "I didn't want to go to that damn party in the first place. I knew something like this would happen."

"I thought the reason was that you didn't want to go without me," she said evenly.

"I *didn't*! Why are you trying to twist my words around?"

"Why are you getting so upset?" she countered. "I was merely asking about your evening."

"Only the part I spent with Alicia—and interrogation is a better description."

"I'm sorry you feel pressured," she said coldly. "If you don't want to talk about her, that's fine with me."

Morgan swore under his breath. "I'll never understand this fixation you have over Alicia. Okay, I danced with her. Is that such a crime? I assure you it will never happen again."

"Don't be childish." Her mouth thinned.

"Look who's talking!" he said explosively. Without another word he stormed out of the room.

Stephanie was as angry as he at first. Gradually her anger was replaced by misery. Why had she provoked a confrontation in spite of all her good intentions? The mere mention of Alicia's name caused antagonism between them. Morgan denied any lingering attachment to her, but he must feel something or he wouldn't be so defensive. Maybe he was trying to fool himself.

He returned an hour later with a large tray. Among the silver covers was a crystal vase with a beautiful red rose. After setting the tray down he approached the bed carrying the rose.

"Will you forgive me?" he asked solemnly.

Her heavy heart lifted. "If you'll do the same for me."

He sat on the edge of the bed and took her in his arms. "I should have realized you felt miserable. That was a fine way to cheer up a sick person."

"I didn't have to snap at you," she murmured.

"You didn't, it was the other way around." He smoothed her hair gently. "I don't even know what started the argument."

Stephanie tightened her arms around his neck. "Don't try to remember."

"I won't. I hate it when we argue."

"Let's promise never to do it again."

He chuckled. "That's a little unrealistic. Let's just promise we'll always make up this fast."

"How about in half an hour instead of an hour?"

"An even better idea." He smiled.

She drew back to look at him searchingly. "I don't know what I'd do if anything serious came between us."

"Nothing will," he soothed.

Stephanie was absolutely determined never to let Alicia bother her again. She'd made the vow before, but this time she meant to keep it. The resolution was tested sooner than she expected, since Alicia became a frequent visitor at the castle.

Stephanie's cold had cleared up in a week, and she'd gone back to her old routine. A lot of work had piled up in her absence, so she stayed later than usual. It was an unpleasant surprise to find Lydia and Alicia on the front steps when she returned home after her first day back at the office.

"Alicia was waiting to say hello to you, but we'd almost given up," Lydia said. "There must be some powerful attraction at that ministry office. Are you trying to make Phillipe jealous?" she asked archly.

Stephanie was too annoyed to answer. She turned to the visitor instead. "Hello, Alicia, it's nice to see you."

"Are you feeling better?" Alicia asked.

"Much. It was only a cold."

"They can make you wretched, though."

Lydia waited impatiently for the pleasantries to be over before announcing, "Alicia is helping me redecorate my sitting room."

"I didn't know you were a decorator," Stephanie said to the other woman.

"I'm not, really. I just dabble a little." Alicia smiled ruefully. "I don't know what she wants me for. Lydia doesn't need an amateur to advise her."

"I won't let you back out now," Lydia warned. "You promised to take me to that place that did your draperies."

Alicia looked so ambivalent that Stephanie laughed. "You might as well resign yourself. Lydia always gets what she wants."

"I only hope she doesn't hold me responsible if things don't turn out the way she expects," Alicia answered.

"They will," Lydia said confidently.

Stephanie actually felt sorry for Alicia in the weeks that followed. She knew how demanding Lydia could be. Alicia's sporty red convertible became a familiar sight parked in the driveway.

Stephanie's sympathy dried up when she found Alicia having cocktails with Morgan one afternoon. They were laughing together in a relaxed manner.

"Come and join us," he said. "Lydia went to get one of her endless fabric samples. She'll be back in a minute. What can I fix you to drink?"

"Something in a tall glass," Stephanie answered, although she didn't really want a drink.

"You both must be heartily sick of seeing me here," Alicia remarked.

"Not at all," Stephanie replied politely.

"When I agreed to help Lydia with one room, I had no idea it was only the tip of the iceberg," Alicia said plaintively. "She's talking about redoing the whole apartment."

"Have you ever tried saying no to her?" Stephanie asked with more bluntness than she meant to show.

"How far have *you* gotten with that tactic?" Morgan laughed.

"She has a forceful personality," Stephanie admitted.

The object of their discussion appeared in the doorway. "I didn't know you'd be home so early, Stephanie." Lydia glanced nervously from her to Morgan. "Alicia and I just wanted to measure Phillipe's couch. I think it's the perfect size for the long wall in Henri's bedroom."

"Take all the time you need. Stephanie and I have a date to walk the dogs." Morgan took her hand and led her out the door.

"Wasn't that a little rude?" Stephanie asked, although she was secretly delighted.

"I can see them anytime. You're the one I don't see enough of." He put his arm around her shoulders and hugged her close.

Stephanie rushed into Morgan's office one day shortly afterward. "Guess what? I've been asked to be on the delegation to the World Trade Conference in Paris," she announced breathlessly.

"That's a real honor," he exclaimed. "I'm proud of you, angel."

"Can you go with me? We could stay on after for a vacation."

"I wish I could, but it comes at a bad time for me," he said reluctantly. "I have the foreign ministers' meeting that week."

Her face fell. "Wouldn't you know it? I was hoping we could have a few days alone together."

"What did you have in mind?" He smiled.

"What I always do," she answered demurely.

His lips grazed hers as he murmured, "We don't have to go away for that."

His deep kiss was very satisfying, but she sighed afterward. "It won't be the same without you."

"I certainly hope not." He chuckled. "How long will you be gone?"

"Only three days, unless I meet a passionate Frenchman who has more time for me than my husband."

"Pick one who likes to live dangerously, because it would be his last affair."

Stephanie was filled with excitement over her trip. In a way it became more important because she would be completely on her own. Even Lydia was impressed by the honor. She emerged from her decorating frenzy to ask questions and suggest she stay longer to shop.

The conference was everything Stephanie could have wished. After her initial nervousness over speaking in front of such a distinguished forum, she gained confidence. The acceptance of her colleagues was like champagne in her veins.

She returned home still fizzing like a rocket about to take off.

"I wish you'd been there," she told Morgan. "It was so stimulating. I never had people listen to me like that before."

He smiled. "How am I going to keep you in Verlaine after the bright lights of Paris?"

"That won't be difficult. It lacked one important thing." She put her arms around his neck. "Did you miss me?"

"You better believe it," he murmured huskily.

"What did you do while I was gone?"

"Took a lot of cold showers." He eased her down onto the bed.

Stephanie had only been away from home for three days, but their reunion was torrid enough to make up for a month's separation. She stayed in bed after he left in the morning to savor the memory of their night together.

After a long, luxurious bath she dressed in jeans and loafers, happily contemplating a day of leisure.

"I've been neglecting you, baby, but today we're going to play," she told the big black poodle.

He wagged his short tail with the round pom-pom on the end and barked as though he understood her.

As she was pulling a heavy sweater over her head, one of the maids appeared in the doorway and paused hesitantly.

"I'm sorry, Your Highness," she apologized. "I didn't know you were still here."

Stephanie smiled. "I'm a little late this morning, but you can come in now, Ilsa."

"Thank you, ma'am." The woman handed her a square of pink silk with a flowered border. "I brought your scarf back."

Stephanie had never seen it before. In one corner was a deeper pink monogram: A.Le.B. "Where did you find this?" she asked with a sense of foreboding.

"It was in the wastebasket in His Highness's bedroom. It's so beautiful. I knew you must have thrown it out by mistake."

Stephanie's first reaction was a deep sense of betrayal. It was followed by blinding rage. How dare Morgan humiliate her like this? Without stopping to think, she raced down the stairs to his office and flung open the door. Morgan was sitting at his desk working on some papers.

"What was Alicia doing in our bedroom?" she demanded without preamble.

His welcoming smile changed to a frown. "I don't know what you're talking about."

"Don't try to deny it. I have the evidence right here." She flung the scarf on the desk.

He picked it up curiously. "Is this supposed to mean something to me?"

"Look at the monogram," she ordered.

"It's Alicia's. So what?" He acted genuinely puzzled.

"So Ilsa found it in our room. How did it get there?"

"How in God's name would I know? Maybe Lydia took her up there to measure the furniture. She's invaded every other room in the place."

"Really, Morgan, is that the best you can do?"

His eyes glinted dangerously. "Exactly what are you accusing me of? Entertaining Alicia in our apartment? Making love to her in our bed?"

Stephanie felt sick inside. Would he actually do that? "I'm merely asking for an explanation," she said more calmly.

"That's not what it sounded like."

Her jaw set. "Are you going to give me one or not?"

He watched her without expression. "You wouldn't believe me anyway."

"I always have before," she answered bitterly. "You've managed to talk your way out of every corner, but you can scarcely expect me to excuse this flagrant indiscretion."

"What I would expect from you is trust."

"I expected fidelity," she answered witheringly. "It looks as though both of us aimed too high."

He smiled cruelly. "At least we share a common mistake."

Stephanie's heart twisted with pain at his tacit admission of guilt, but she raised her head proudly. "That appears to be all we share."

"Not quite." His gaze traveled insolently over her body. "We have one other common interest."

"You think that makes up for everything?" she exclaimed in outrage.

"We'll have to see, won't we?" He stood up and sauntered out of the room.

Chapter Eleven

Stephanie was utterly crushed after the encounter with Morgan. He hadn't even bothered to put up a defense. Did that mean he didn't care if she divorced him or not? Perhaps even wanted her to? The dreaded word was never mentioned, but how could their marriage survive under the circumstances? She couldn't even bear to sleep in his bed anymore.

She didn't actually believe he'd shared it with Alicia. Morgan might not love her any longer, yet he wouldn't do anything that tawdry. It was his assumption that sex would bring her around that hurt. If all they had between them was a mutual attraction, it wasn't enough.

Stephanie knew she could never remain indifferent to him if they occupied the same bed, so she moved her things into the other bedroom. Her self-respect demanded that much.

Morgan didn't comment on the switch, although she hoped he would come to her with a magic explanation—or even an apology—that would heal the rift. Hadn't they promised to make up swiftly if they quarreled?

On the first night alone in her solitary bed, her heart leaped when she felt a soft thud on the mattress next to her. She turned over eagerly, but it was the poodle, Pepe. He curled up next to her with a sigh of contentment.

She stroked his curly fur as the tears spilled down her cheeks. "Okay, pal, I guess it's just you and me from now on. But I'll take all the love I can get."

Morgan appeared perfectly content with the arrangement, but Stephanie was devastated. They were carefully polite to each other, nothing more. Their sole contact was confined to public appearances they couldn't avoid.

The occasions when they had to dance together were the worst. Morgan's hand on her waist and the shifting shoulder muscles under her fingers were tormenting reminders of a different sort of contact. She searched his face for some sign that he was similarly affected, but his only reaction was cool courtesy.

Before a large gala, Morgan knocked formally on her door. Stephanie was already dressed in a rose-colored lace gown. Something flared for just a second in his eyes as he gazed at the swell of her breasts over the low décolletage, but she was so used to avoiding eye contact that she missed it.

His expression was indifferent by the time he handed her a large blue velvet box. "Your maid told me you were wearing pink. These should go with your outfit."

Inside the case was a dazzling array of rubies and diamonds—a necklace, bracelet, earrings, even a tiara. Stephanie's delight was evident as she stared at the glittering gems, touching them gently.

"They're gorgeous," she murmured.

"You should wear them more often—except for the tiara. That might be a little much for ordinary occasions."

"I always feel nervous about wearing borrowed jewelry," she said diffidently.

"They belong to you."

"No, they're the crown jewels."

Deep lines bracketed Morgan's mouth. "You're my wife, which makes you the Queen of Verlaine."

An inadequate one, judging by his expression. Stephanie masked her hurt with a regal lift of her head. "I'll try to live up to the title in public, anyway."

He gave her a brooding look and left the room without answering.

Stephanie was reaching the breaking point when Morgan informed her that he had to fly to London for a conference.

"You can come with me if you like," he said.

The disinterest in his voice told her it was only a token invitation. "Thanks, but I have a meeting of my own at the same time," she said.

He smiled mirthlessly. "I hope the people realize what dedicated monarchs they have."

Stephanie spent the week he was gone trying to decide what to do. They couldn't go on this way, and any hope for a reconciliation was only wishful thinking. Morgan's acceptance of their way of life was evidence that he no longer cared.

Was it because he'd fallen in love with Alicia again—or fallen out of love with *her*? Did their troubles really begin when they found out they couldn't have children? Morgan had been supportive, but it must have been a bitter disappointment, especially in his circumstances.

He was also a very virile man. If he wasn't already having an affair with Alicia, it was only because of his innate decency. Shouldn't she give him his freedom so he could make a more suitable marriage? Hanging on to him was only making them both miserable.

Stephanie thought she'd made up her mind, but when Morgan returned and she was faced with the actuality of never seeing him again, her resolve weakened. Even though he didn't seem in any hurry to see her. She heard him moving around in his room, but he didn't come looking for her.

When they met a little later his gaze sharpened. "Are you all right? You don't look well."

She'd lost weight, and there were shadows under her eyes from lack of sleep. It didn't help to be told she was turning into a hag, though.

"You've just forgotten what I look like," she said lightly.

"In a week? That's hardly likely." He stared at her broodingly.

She changed the subject. "Did you have a nice trip?"

"Yes, I think it was quite productive."

They discussed government affairs, but Morgan was abstracted. He kept looking at her searchingly.

"I think you ought to see a doctor," he said unexpectedly.

"What for? I'm fine."

His mouth tightened. "Why must you always be so stubborn?"

Stephanie felt suddenly defeated. What was the use? "I just need a vacation. I've been thinking about going to visit my sister." It was a sudden inspiration.

"That might be a good idea," he said slowly. "I can't get away for about ten days, but I'll have Jacques make the reservations."

That would defeat the whole purpose. Stephanie didn't think she could take the strain of pretending that everything was all right in front of her family and friends.

"I didn't expect you to go with me," she said swiftly.

"You mean you don't want me to." His face was austere.

"I didn't say that," she protested.

"But it's what you meant."

"I realize you have more important things to do here," she said carefully.

"Are you giving me your blessing, Stephanie?" He watched her closely.

Her shoulders slumped. "If that's what you want."

"When do you want to leave? I'll have Jacques accompany you."

"I don't want him, either." She bit her lip at the inadvertent admission. "I mean, I don't need anyone to take me. I'm not a child."

"A member of the royal family always travels with an aide," he said coldly.

"I'm not paying a state visit. I'm going home to my family."

They argued, but Stephanie stood firm. Finally Morgan stalked out of the room. Most of their conversations seemed to end that way.

Stephanie and her family enjoyed a joyous reunion, the kind where everyone talks at once and no questions get answered. Finally she and her sister were alone in front of the fireplace. Spenser and the boys had gone to bed.

"It's been so long since we've gotten together like this," Eloise said contentedly. "Your wedding didn't count."

"No, it didn't," Stephanie answered dully. When Eloise looked at her with a slight frown, she said quickly, "That was a time of pure hysteria."

Her sister smiled reminiscently. "It was fun, though. My
rst and undoubtedly last time on television."

"How did you like being a celebrity?"

"Fame is fleeting," Eloise observed. "They still
xpected me to take my turn in the car pool when I got
ome."

"Life is hard." Stephanie grinned.

"Not for you. Tell me about all the glamourous things
ou've been doing."

"They're only glamourous because they're far away. I
o pretty much the same things you do."

"I don't envy you cleaning all those rooms," Eloise said
ryly.

Stephanie's eyes sparkled mischievously. "I made it
lear from the beginning that I don't do windows."

"Don't be modest. I want to hear how the other half
ives. Start with a typical day."

"You'd be disappointed," Stephanie told her. "I'm a
vorking woman. I spend most of my time at the World
Trade Congress, where they treat me like everybody else."

"I'm impressed. Where did you learn about world
rade? It's a far cry from Miss Waycroft's."

"Everything is," Stephanie answered somberly. "I
lidn't realize I was living in a cocoon there. It's a wonder
he girls can survive in the real world when they gradu-
ite."

"Is something wrong?" Eloise asked tentatively.

Stephanie recovered quickly. She'd resolved not to dump
ler troubles on anyone, even her sister. Nobody could
olve them but herself. "Are you kidding? I'm a queen.
How can you top that?"

"Not when you're married to a man like Morgan,"
Eloise agreed, relaxing. "Besides being gorgeous, he
idores you. I'm surprised he let you out of his sight for
his long. How long *are* you staying, incidentally?"

"I just got here. Are you trying to get rid of me already?" Stephanie smiled.

"You know better than that. What I really want to know is if Morgan is coming. Our friends and neighbors have been dying to meet him."

"Morgan is awfully tied up at the moment," Stephanie said vaguely.

"Well, if he does come I hope he won't mind being put on display." Eloise laughed. "Otherwise I'd have to move out of the neighborhood."

Stephanie's days and nights were packed with activity. Everyone wanted to see her again and satisfy their curiosity about Verlaine. That was the bad part. They asked endless questions, which only poured salt in her wounds. She'd hoped, foolishly, to forget her problems for a while.

She'd also hoped that Morgan would telephone. When a week went by without any word from him, it became embarrassing.

"Feel free to call your husband. We'll frame the bill as a souvenir of our connection with royalty," Spenser joked.

"A considerate guest pays her own phone bills, and all I have are pictures of Morgan on funny money," Stephanie joked back.

It finally became apparent to Eloise that something was wrong. She gave Stephanie every opportunity to confide in her, and when that didn't work she took direct action.

They had come home from dinner at a restaurant. As Spenser yawned and said good-night, Stephanie started for her own room, but Eloise stopped her.

"Are you really sleepy? Let's talk for a while," she suggested.

Stephanie had a premonition. "It's late, and we're all talked out."

"Not completely. Come in the living room with me," Eloise said adamantly.

Stephanie's feet lagged as she followed her sister. "We won't have anything to say at breakfast besides good morning," she protested feebly.

"Is something wrong between you and Morgan?" Eloise went right to the heart of the matter.

"Whatever gave you that idea?" Stephanie pretended surprise.

"Perhaps the fact that you haven't been in contact for over a week."

"Is that all? Good heavens, he's thousands of miles away."

"Did you two develop some kind of religious objection to using the telephone?"

"The connections are usually bad, and the time difference is a pain. Who can make sense at six o'clock in the morning?"

"What's wrong, Stephanie?" Eloise cut through her lame excuses. "Are you and Morgan having problems? Is this really just a visit, or have you left him?"

"I don't know." Stephanie dropped the pretense that everything was rosy.

"What kind of an answer is that? Either you have or you haven't."

"I *should* leave him, but I can't seem to make the break final." Stephanie sighed. "Maybe Morgan is doing it for me."

"What happened?" Eloise asked urgently.

"He doesn't love me anymore," Stephanie answered simply.

"I can't believe that! You haven't even been married a year."

"What does that have to do with it? Marriage isn't necessarily a long-term contract. When one person wants out, the other person should release him."

"Is there another woman?" Eloise asked quietly.

"That's part of it."

Eloise frowned. "I can understand being upset over infidelity. What could share equal billing?"

"I can't blame Morgan for all our problems," Stephanie explained carefully. "Perhaps he felt justified since I can't give him what he needs."

After a short silence Eloise said hesitantly, "Have you considered having sex counseling?"

Stephanie's smile was twisted. "That's the only area where we don't need any help."

"Then I don't understand."

"It's very simple. I can't give Morgan children."

After she'd listened to the whole story, Eloise looked stricken. "I'm so sorry," she whispered.

Stephanie nodded. "Now you can see why I have to let Morgan go."

"No, I don't. It's terribly sad, but you didn't get married just to have children."

"Then why did he lose interest in me after he found out?"

"You indicated that he hasn't lost interest completely. Are you sure there's another woman?"

"She's practically living with us," Stephanie said bitterly.

Eloise expressed shock. "He brings her to the house?"

"No, she has a good reason for being there." Stephanie explained Alicia's friendship with the family and the reason for her constant presence. "I will say Alicia didn't want to take on the job, but Lydia wouldn't let her off the hook. Morgan was annoyed at first because they kept invading his office."

Eloise looked thoughtful. "I presume Lydia knew about the affair he and Alicia once had?"

"Everyone in Verlaine seems to have known."

"Did you ever get the impression that Lydia would have preferred Alicia as a sister-in-law?"

"Lydia didn't want Morgan to marry anyone. She told me so. But she's resigned to the fact now."

"Is she? Or was she hoping this very situation would develop if he and Alicia were thrown together regularly?"

"That's ridiculous. Lydia is insensitive, I'll grant you, but setting Morgan up with another woman doesn't make sense. What good would it do her to break up my marriage if he simply turned around and married Alicia?"

"I imagine she planned to deal with that after she got rid of you."

"You can't really think she's such a monster!" Stephanie exclaimed.

"I got the impression of a woman with enormous ambition and no way to satisfy it. That's a dangerous combination."

"But I'm not the one standing in her way, Morgan is."

"Exactly. If something happened to him, Henri would succeed to the throne."

"You're not honestly suggesting that Lydia would try to harm Morgan?"

"No, that isn't as easy to get away with as it was in the days of the Borgias. But accidents happen all the time. Planes go down, people get killed in high-risk sports. The idea is to keep him single, so if he does die, he won't leave any heirs."

Stephanie's eyes were shadowed. "If that was her plan, she'd be better off if he stayed married to me."

Eloise frowned. "Does Lydia know you can't have children?"

Stephanie shook her head. "I couldn't talk about it."

"I understand." Eloise patted her hand in sympathy. "It must have been a blow to both of you."

"Morgan took it better than I did at first. When I offered him a divorce he said he'd abdicate before he'd let me go." Stephanie's voice was wistful.

"I wonder," Eloise murmured, gazing at her sister with concentration. "Something just occurred to me. Did you ever think of having your condition confirmed by another doctor?"

"What's the use?" Stephanie asked drearily. "I'd just be torturing myself with foolish hope. Lydia says Dr. Courbet is the most eminent gynecologist in Verlaine."

"Lydia's name keeps popping up a little too often," Eloise muttered. "How did you happen to go to this oracle of wisdom?"

"Lydia sent me," Stephanie answered slowly.

They stared at each other silently. Then Eloise said, "Tomorrow you're going to see the most eminent doctor in Vermont."

Stephanie looked dazed when she came out of the doctor's office the next day. Instead of asking questions, Eloise drove her home.

When they were seated at the kitchen table with steaming cups of coffee she said, "Do you feel like talking about it?"

"I think so." Tears welled up in Stephanie's eyes.

"You don't have to if it's too difficult. Why didn't I listen to you?" Eloise lamented. "I'll never forgive myself for putting you through this again."

"No, it's all right. He said I could have a baby—a dozen babies—unlimited babies!" Stephanie was laughing and crying at the same time.

"You mean there's nothing wrong with you?"

"Not exactly. I need some minor corrective surgery, but after that I'll be fine."

"Oh, Steffie, that's wonderful news!" The sisters hugged joyously. "You have to tell Morgan immediately," Eloise declared. "What time is it there? Oh, what's the matter with me? What difference does it make? Call him!"

"I don't want to tell him over the phone." Stephanie pleated her skirt nervously. "I don't even know if I should tell him at all."

"Why on earth not? You just received the best possible news. Why would you keep it from your husband?"

"It might be too late to make any difference."

"You don't really believe that," Eloise chided.

"I've been gone for over a week, and he hasn't even sent me a postcard. Does that sound as though he wants me back?"

"You've had a series of misunderstandings. These things build up. Morgan is probably giving you time to cool off."

"Or else he's enjoying his freedom."

"Call him," Eloise urged. "I'll bet he's as miserable as you are."

"I don't know," Stephanie said doubtfully.

"Are you going to let your marriage break up because you're too proud to make the first move? That's just what Lydia's counting on," Eloise added craftily.

Her ploy worked. Stephanie's eyes turned to green ice as she remembered the pain her sister-in-law had caused. She picked up the telephone and dialed long distance.

Maurice the butler answered. After an exchange of pleasantries he said, "His Highness is attending a party in Prince Henri's apartment. I'll send someone to tell him you're calling."

"Wait, Maurice! Do you know who...I suppose it's some kind of bachelor party."

"No, ma'am. Princess Lydia called it a housewarming, I believe. She's displaying her new furnishings."

"I see."

"I'll get His Highness for you."

"Don't bother," Stephanie said dully. "I mean, I'll call back later. And Maurice—don't tell His Highness I phoned. I, uh, I want to surprise him."

"What was that all about?" Eloise asked after she'd hung up.

"My suffering spouse is drowning his sorrows in champagne—with Alicia."

"How do you know that?"

"Lydia's intriguing hand again. She's having a party."

"That doesn't mean Alicia is there."

"It's in her honor. Or maybe it's a victory celebration." Stephanie's eyes were bleak. "What difference does it make? This shoots down your miserable Morgan theory, anyway."

Eloise hid her chagrin. "You mustn't overreact. People don't necessarily show their unhappiness by staying home and moping. *You've* been going out."

"With you and Spenser. That's a little different from living it up with a former love."

Eloise gave her a troubled look. "What do you plan to do?"

"Since I don't have anything pressing on my calendar, this seems like a good time to take care of my little medical problem. That's *one* problem I can solve, anyway," Stephanie said grimly.

Morgan sat on Lydia's new couch and stared morosely into his drink, wondering how he'd let her talk him into attending this asinine affair. He was deciding to leave when Alicia sat down next to him.

"You evidently don't approve of my efforts," she remarked.

"On the contrary. I think you did an excellent job," he answered politely.

"Tell me what color the walls are—without looking," she added.

Morgan smiled. "I'm afraid I'm one of those men who never notice things like that."

"Most men don't. They can never see that anything needs doing over."

"Did Henri object? Not that it would have done him any good."

"Henri has a wonderful attitude," Alicia replied diplomatically.

"It's called peace at any price."

"That sounds rather harsh," she protested. "Some things simply aren't worth arguing over."

"You're right, there are enough other things," Morgan muttered.

After a quick look at his set face, Alicia changed the subject. "I suppose Stephanie is having a wonderful time with her family. When is she coming home?"

"I have no idea," he answered morosely. When Alicia looked uncomfortable he attempted to pass it off as a joke. "I suppose when she and her sister run out of things to talk about—which could take all winter."

"I'm sure she couldn't stay away from you that long."

Morgan let his unhappiness show. "You have more confidence than I."

"That's because I recognize love when I see it. You two have the kind of relationship I've been looking for all my life."

"You'll find it some day," he said gently.

"I thought I had, but there was never any chance for us, was there?"

He chose his words carefully. "We had something very rare between a man and a woman—true friendship. I'd like to think we'll always be friends."

Her laughter had a catch in it. "That's like winning the title of Miss Congeniality when you really wanted the crown."

"I'm sorry," he said quietly.

"I am, too." She smiled gallantly. "Tell Stephanie to stop being such a chump. People who have everything and don't know it are very annoying."

Morgan went back to his own quarters after the conversation. Pepe greeted him with the restrained enthusiasm poodles allow themselves at happy moments, but Morgan didn't share his pleasure.

"Don't pretend you're glad to see me," he told the big dog moodily. "You're just lonesome. That makes two of us," he muttered, sitting down on the foot of the bed.

When Pepe put his chin on Morgan's knee, he stroked the dog's head. "I suppose you think I should call her." A long moment went by while his longing wrestled with his pride. He stood up abruptly as pride won out.

"No, damn it! Why should I grovel? I haven't done anything. If she doesn't trust me, what's the use?"

Stephanie was looking out the hospital window at the gray sky, which matched her mood. When Eloise came in with a bunch of flowers she forced a smile.

"How are you feeling?" Eloise asked.

"Great. I'm taking up this bed under false pretenses."

"The doctor wants you to stay for a couple of days simply for observation. Spenser sends his love."

"He's a dear. I hope I haven't complicated your lives too much. I'll be out of your hair soon."

"We love having you. What else do I have to do with the boys in school all day?"

"I'm sure you could find something more rewarding."

"I can't think of anything." Eloise gazed fondly at her sister. "You've made me a celebrity by association."

"Fortunately you have other assets to fall back on."

Eloise's face sobered. "You haven't changed your mind about telling Morgan?"

"I've been concerned with other things."

"Of course you have, but the doctor says you're just fine."

"That's nice," Stephanie answered neutrally.

Morgan spent a restless night. He tossed and turned so much that Pepe finally climbed down from the bed in disgust.

When light started to seep through the edges of the heavy draperies, Morgan got out of bed. He showered and shaved, staring in the mirror with a deep scowl. The days were long enough without starting them at six o'clock.

He reviewed the appointments on his calendar and found them boring. Nothing interested him anymore. He stared into his own eyes and realized that pride carried too high a price. Somehow, some way, he'd have to convince Stephanie that they belonged together.

Once the decision was made he felt revitalized. Excitement flowed through his veins as he listened to the phone ring.

An unfamiliar female voice answered. "Her ladyship isn't here," the woman told him.

Morgan's disappointment was intense. "Then let me speak to Mrs. Farrell."

"She isn't here either."

"When will they be back?"

"Mrs. Farrell won't be home until five. She had some errands to do after she visits her sister in the hospital. I won't be here then, but I can leave her a message if you like.''

"What hospital? What are you talking about?'' Morgan's heart contracted with dread. "Has there been an accident?''

"I'm just the cleaning lady, mister. I don't know any more than I told you.''

Morgan tried to control his panic as he made swift arrangements to fly to Vermont. It helped to have something to do, but underneath his crisp efficiency was a feeling of desolation. How could he go on living if anything happened to Stephanie?

Spenser was in bed and Eloise was getting undressed when the doorbell rang. They looked at each other blankly. Who could it be at such a late hour?

Eloise put on a robe and went downstairs. She looked cautiously through the peephole in the front door, but since the porch light was burned out all she could see was two large men. It wasn't a reassuring sight.

"Who is it?'' she asked with some apprehension.

"It's Morgan, let me in,'' he called impatiently.

Eloise hastily opened the door. "Thank God you're here!''

He paled. "Stephanie isn't . . .'' He couldn't voice the unspeakable.

"Come in.'' She looked curiously at Morgan's aide, but he didn't introduce Jacques.

Morgan was too driven. "Tell me she's alive,'' he begged.

"Of course she's alive! Whatever gave you the idea she wasn't?''

"I phoned this morning and some woman told me Stephanie was in the hospital. What happened? Why wasn't I told?''

"It isn't anything serious," Eloise answered evasively.

"People don't go to the hospital for minor ailments. What are you keeping from me?"

"Let's go in the living room and sit down. I'll make coffee."

"I want to know what's wrong with Stephanie," he said forcefully.

"She needed a slight operation, that's all. It's nothing to be concerned about."

"You expect me to believe that? She was fine when she left home."

"She's even better now," Eloise said soothingly. "You can see her in the morning, and she'll tell you all about it."

"I want to see her *now*! What hospital is she in?"

"They won't let you in at this hour."

Jacques had stayed in the background, waiting until he was needed. His concerned expression turned into a little smile. She evidently didn't know Morgan very well.

He usually got his way through a mixture of charm and veiled authority, but Morgan was too distracted that night to use either. Force was on his mind when the desk nurse at the hospital refused him permission to see Stephanie. It was Jacques who tactfully explained the situation. Morgan was allowed to go to Stephanie's room merely to look at her. He had to promise not to wake her.

She wasn't asleep. As the door clicked open with a muted sound she turned her head listlessly, expecting a nurse. At first she thought she'd been asleep after all, and Morgan was a figment of her dreams.

"Morgan?" she asked uncertainly. When he approached the bed her doubts vanished. Every coordinated movement of that lithe frame was familiar to her. "What are you doing here?"

"I came as soon as I heard you were in the hospital."

"How did you find out?"

"It doesn't matter. What happened? Nobody will tell me." His voice was agonized.

Stephanie's heart soared as she gazed at his ravaged face. Even in the dim light the harsh lines were evident. Morgan had dropped everything and flown to her side when he believed she needed him. How could she have thought he'd stopped caring?

"Pull up a chair," she said gently. "This might take a while."

Morgan looked stunned after she'd finished. Joy and anger warred on his strong face. He reached for her hands and held them tightly. "The main thing is that you're all right. I'll settle with Lydia when we get home."

"What are you going to do? She's your brother's wife," she reminded him.

"Let me worry about that. I promise she'll never interfere in our lives again. I don't know how I could have been so blind."

"Circumstances played into her hands. If I could have had a baby without any problem, I never would have been jealous of Alicia. Well, not seriously, anyway." She smiled.

"How could you have had the slightest doubt?"

Stephanie's face sobered. "Lydia was very clever. She fed my suspicion bit by bit, knowing I'd question you about Alicia, and you'd deny any interest in her at first, then get annoyed at my lack of trust. Which would only confirm my conviction that you were still involved with her. It was a vicious circle."

"The woman is diabolical!"

"Also resourceful." Stephanie nodded. "I have no doubt that Lydia planted that scarf in your wastebasket as the clincher."

"Did you honestly believe I was having an affair with Alicia?"

"No, but I thought you wanted to," Stephanie answered honestly. "Things had been going from bad to worse between us, and you didn't deny anything when I forced a showdown."

"I was hurt and angry. I was also a fool," he added remorsefully.

"That makes two of us. What kind of parents are we going to make?" she asked with gentle mockery.

"Very loving ones." He kissed her tenderly.

Morgan not only lifted Stephanie out of the car on their return home, he insisted on carrying her all the way up the stairs.

"You're treating me like an invalid," she objected. "The doctor said I'm perfectly fine."

"I could have told him that, only I'd have used more glowing terms."

"Seriously, darling, he told me I should lead a normal life."

Morgan set her on her feet beside the bed, but he didn't release her. "Does that include sharing a room with someone other than a poodle?" he murmured.

"That certainly sounds normal to me." She lifted her face invitingly.

Their kiss expressed all the pent-up passion they had denied during the weeks of misunderstandings. Morgan's hungry mouth feasted on her lips, her neck, burrowed inside her blouse.

She was compliant as he undressed her, melting before the flame in his eyes as he touched her breasts almost reverently. The feathery strokes were so erotic that she gasped with pleasure.

"I thought I'd only imagined you were this beautiful, but I was wrong," he said thickly. "You're even more exquisite than I remembered."

"I never forgot anything about you."

She wrapped her arms around his chest and pressed closely against him, kneading the corded muscles through his shirt. Morgan stroked her bare back with the same rhythm. When his hands cupped around her buttocks she pulled his shirt out of his slacks.

"I missed you so," she whispered.

"We'll make up for every lonely hour," he promised, lifting her tenderly onto the bed.

Their passion was too urgent to be drawn out. It escalated swiftly, climaxing in a burst of nerve-tightening sensation that was shared by their closely locked bodies. Afterward they remained clasped in each other's arms, whispering muted words of love.

Stephanie was drifting off to sleep when Morgan eased out of her arms. "Where are you going?" she asked.

"I have something to do."

"Come back to me," she murmured as her lashes fluttered down.

He chuckled softly. "Don't worry, I will."

Henri sat across the desk from Morgan, his face a mask of consternation. "I had no idea. To say I'm sorry is woefully inadequate."

"I realize you had no part in this."

"That doesn't excuse me. I should have paid more attention to her. I never questioned Lydia because it was easier for *me*. Perhaps if I'd been more authoritative she wouldn't be so insecure. That's what this bid for power is all about."

Morgan looked skeptical. "Possibly, but her intrigue almost ruined my life. You can understand why I'm not too sympathetic."

"Of course. We'll be out of here tomorrow."

"Unfortunately, that's the only solution." Morgan looked at his younger brother with regret. "I'm sorry for our sake, but your life won't change that radically."

"That's where you're wrong." Henri's usually smiling mouth set in a firm line. "I'm thirty-four years old. It's time I grew up and became the head of my household. Which includes going to work instead of being a perennial playboy."

"I certainly approve of that. Do you have any idea what you'd like to do?"

Henri grinned, his intensity diluted by his natural good humor. "That's a tough one. I'm not exactly shot through with talent."

"Don't sell yourself short." Morgan looked thoughtful. "You have a natural talent for people."

"Social skills aren't in great demand."

"They are in the diplomatic corps. How would you like to be Verlaine's ambassador to America?"

"Couldn't you choose a smaller country? A superpower will strike back if Lydia starts a war."

"I'm serious," Morgan assured him. "How about it?"

Henri looked slightly dazed as the idea took hold. "Do you really think I could handle it?"

"Piece of cake. They love titles over there. Lydia will finally have her own court."

The brothers discussed ways and means, with Henri becoming more and more excited. By the time they parted he was like a new man.

Morgan was filled with quiet satisfaction at the change in his brother. It was something he'd given up hope of ever seeing. At least something good had come out of a near tragedy.

As he removed his clothes once more and slipped into bed next to his sleeping wife, Morgan forgot all about Henri.

Epilogue

It was eleven months later that Stephanie and Morgan stepped onto the balcony to display their son to his future subjects. The courtyard was crowded with smiling people craning for a better look at the sleeping infant. Morgan's pride was evident as he gazed adoringly at his wife and child.

"I do wish he'd wake up so everybody can see he has your blue eyes," Stephanie fretted. "It might make up for the fact that he inherited my auburn hair."

"Maybe the next baby will have dark hair if that's what you want," he consoled her.

"Aren't you rushing things a bit?"

"I only want to make you happy, my love." His smile was mischievous.

"You have, darling," she answered softly. "So very happy."

He kissed her tenderly, to the delight of the crowd.

* * * * *

Silhouette Special Edition®

presents

LOVE AND GLORY

from
Lindsay McKenna

Introducing a gripping new series celebrating our men—and women—in uniform. Meet the Trayherns, a military family as proud and colorful as the American flag, a family fighting the shadow of dishonor, a family determined to triumph—with
LOVE AND GLORY!

June: A QUESTION OF HONOR (SE #529) leads the fast-paced excitement. When Coast Guard officer Noah Trayhern offers Kit Anderson a safe house, he unwittingly endangers his own guarded emotions.

July: NO SURRENDER (SE #535) Navy pilot Alyssa Trayhern's assignment with arrogant jet jockey Clay Cantrell threatens her career—and her heart—with a crash landing!

August: RETURN OF A HERO (SE #541) Strike up the band to welcome home a man whose top-secret reappearance will make headline news . . . with a delicate, daring woman by his side.

Silhouette Special Edition

COMING NEXT MONTH

#535 NO SURRENDER—Lindsay McKenna
Navy pilot Alyssa Trayhern's assignment with arrogant jet jockey
Clay Cantrell threatens her pride, her career—and her heart—with a
crash landing. Book Two of Lindsay McKenna's gripping LOVE
AND GLORY series.

#536 A TENDER SILENCE—Karen Keast
Former POW Kell Chaisson knew all about survival. He'd brave
Bangkok's dangers to help Anne Elise Butler trace her MIA
husband's fate, but would he survive loving another man's wife?

#537 THORNE'S WIFE—Joan Hohl
Jonas Thorne was accomplished, powerful, devastatingly attractive.
Valerie Thorne loved her husband, but what would it take to convince
domineering Jonas that she was a person, not simply his wife?

#538 LIGHT FOR ANOTHER NIGHT—Anne Lacey
Wildlife biologist Brittany Hagen loved the wolves on primeval Isle
Svenson...until she encountered the two-legged variety—in the
person of ferociously attractive, predatory Paul Johnson.

#539 EMILY'S HOUSE—Nikki Benjamin
Vowing to secretly support widowed Emily Anderson and her child,
Major Joseph Cortez rented rooms in her house. But, hiding a guilty
secret, could he ever gain entrance to Emily's heart?

#540 LOVE THIS STRANGER—Linda Shaw
Pregnant nutritionist Mary Smith unwittingly assumed another
woman's identity when she accepted a job with the Olympic ski team.
Worse, she also "inherited" devastating Dr. Jed Kilpatrick—the
other woman's lover!

AVAILABLE THIS MONTH: